FIRST WEDDING, ONCE REMOVED

BY THE AUTHOR OF

Say Goodnight, Gracie
You Bet Your Life

First Wedding, Once Removed

Julie Reece Deaver

A Charlotte Zolotow Book

HarperTrophy
A Division of HarperCollins*Publishers*

Library of Congress Cataloging-in-Publication Data
Deaver, Julie Reece.
  First wedding, once removed / by Julie Reece Deaver.
    p. cm.
  "A Charlotte Zolotow book."
  Summary: Depicts thirteen-year-old Pokie's friendship with her
older brother and the changes it undergoes when her brother falls in
love.
  ISBN 0-06-021426-0. — ISBN 0-06-021427-9 (lib. bdg.)
  ISBN 0-06-440402-1 (pbk.)
  [1. Brothers and sisters—Fiction. 2. Friendship—Fiction.] I. Title.
PZ7.D3524Fi 1990   90-4184
[Fic]—dc20   CIP
                                                                  AC

First Harper Trophy edition, 1993.

*for Alwilda Reece and Wilds Pembroke
(otherwise known as Dee and Danny),
for Ethel and Nelson
and Jeffery*

*with appreciation to my technical advisor
Colonel (Ret.) F. E. "Rox" Schneider*

and special thanks to Nancy Jewell Geller

Part One

1

Picture if you will a brilliant summer's day, a still day, its hazy greenery shimmering in the sun like a scene from one of those glossy-paged fairy-tale books.

"Ah," I hear over and over, "what a day for the wedding!"

The wedding. I am fourteen years old and sister of the groom. I am also the head bridesmaid in this wedding and the only calm person in a house full of wrecks.

"Pokie," says my mother from the next room, "what are you up to? Don't sit down or you'll wrinkle your dress."

"I'm not sitting down!" I holler.

"What?"

"I said I'm not sitting down!"

What I'm doing is standing in front of the full-length mirror, studying myself in this lime-green monstrosity Nell has picked out for her bridesmaids. I situate the bridesmaid hat on my head and do the best I can with the dress—try to squash some of the puff out of the sleeves and smooth down the ruffles—but it's no use: All Nell's taste is in her mouth.

My mother appears in the doorway. "Very nice," she says. "But puff up those sleeves! And go help Nell; she's having trouble with her zipper."

"I'm afraid people will laugh at me when I walk down the aisle," I say. "This is the ugliest dress I've ever witnessed."

My mother smiles. "No one will laugh at you. I think maybe you're just not accustomed to wearing something with ruffles on it."

"Oh." I take another look at myself in the mirror. "By the way . . . I'll be fifteen next year. I think it's time everybody started calling me Alwilda."

"Your brother's the one who nicknamed you Pokie," my mother says. "Maybe you should talk to him."

"Maybe I will," I say. I slip into my new high-heeled shoes, purchased on sale at Shoe-A-Rama. I teeter in them when I walk, like Minnie Mouse when she dances with Mickey. I clack down the hall to the room that used to be mine before Nell took it over. I knock on the door.

"Pokie?" I hear Nell say.

I open the door. "I'm trying to get everyone to call me by my right name, which is Alwilda, in case you didn't know."

"Alwilda . . . is that a family name?"

"I was named for my great-great-grandmother. She smoked a pipe and got arrested for making birth-control speeches."

"Really? How interesting."

"Hell, hasn't Gib told you anything about our family?"

"I guess we just haven't had time to learn everything about each other's families yet."

I turn her around and start tugging at the zipper. Nell is being married in my mother's wedding dress. Up until last week the gown had been carefully packed away in the attic. For me. For the day I get married.

"Too bad your mother didn't send you *her* wedding gown," I say.

"What? Oh . . . my mama didn't get married in a wedding gown. She wore a blue seersucker suit, white shoes, and a white hat with cherries on it. She got married on her lunch break from the Kansas City Power and Light Company."

This is a lot more than I want to know about Nell's mother's wedding. I give the zipper a good hard yank and it glides up the dress on its track.

Nell picks up the skirts of the dress and turns around. "How do I look?"

Nell is beautiful: She stands by the window and the sun softly silhouettes her in the ivory lace gown. She whirls around and there's a rustle of taffeta against starched crinoline underskirts.

"You look like the cover of one of those brides' magazines I've seen down at the drugstore."

She smiles and picks a lipstick up off the dressing table and paints her lips without even looking in the mirror. She holds the lipstick out to me. "Want some?"

I take the lipstick from her and look at it: *Bargain Big Top's Posy Pink.* I try putting it on without looking but end up getting it all over my mouth. Nell laughs and dabs at my face with her hankie.

"Makeup takes a little practice," she says. "You can keep it if you want."

"No," I say. I wipe my mouth with the back of my hand. "I think I'll go plain. I hate the way girls go around worrying about how their makeup looks all the time."

Nell glances in the mirror and fluffs her bangs. She picks up a bottle of Charlie and sprays her wrists. She reaches over and sprays my wrists, too. "Well? Did you ever think a year ago you'd be getting yourself a sister-in-law?"

"No," I say. "No, I never did."

———

Things were a lot different last summer.
Things were a lot different before Nell.

Before there was Gib and Nell, there was Gib and me.

2

Last summer Gib didn't even know Nell existed. Last summer started the way it always had: me up at the crack of dawn, rushing into Gib's room and yanking the pillow out from under his head.

"Wake up!" I said. "C'mon, Gib . . . it's summer!"

"Seven! Lord, Poke, what'd you wake me up for? You know I was out practically all night at that graduation party—"

"Oh, shoot, you were not. You came in at one thirty. I heard you."

"I've got a hangover! Leave me alone!"

I pulled the blanket down to his chin. "Who you trying to kid? You didn't drink anything, I'll bet—"

"Only about ten cases of beer, that's all." He grabbed the pillow from me and stuffed it under his head. He shut his eyes. "Why don't you go next door and play with Junior Hollinger or something?"

"I can play with him anytime," I said. "Come on, Gib. . . . I thought we could go out to Mitchell Field and watch the planes land like we did last summer—"

"Maybe later."

"Heck, I never thought I'd see the day when you'd rather sleep than go to an airfield."

Gib's whole room, in fact, looks like a miniature airfield: Model airplanes are suspended from the ceiling by thin wires; he has a poster of the instrument panel of a Piper Cub taped to his wall; he even has the busted landing gear of a Cessna 152 propped against his closet door to keep it shut. On his dresser is the green china airplane bank I made him in art class. Gib's going to be a pilot someday, and the first time he solos, he's promised to fly low over our house and circle it twice so I know it's him.

"Well, seems like some people don't care *how* bored their sisters got last night at that god-awful graduation," I said in a loud voice. "I could have stayed home watching 'The Amazing Colossal Man' on *Science Fiction Theater*, but I thought your graduation was more important."

Gib opened his eyes. "All right, Pokie. Okay.

9

You better go downstairs and pack us a big lunch; we'll probably be out there all day."

"I will," I said. "Hurry up, okay? We don't want to miss anything. . . ."

I raced down to the kitchen and almost ran right into my mother.

"Hey, hold on there, Speed Demon!" she said. She was standing in her rumpled old robe and had the coffeepot in her hand. "Where you off to in such a hurry? I thought you'd be sleeping late this morning."

"Gib and I are going out to the airfield," I said. "I have to pack us a lunch."

"Pokie . . . you woke him up? He didn't get in till all hours last night—"

"He doesn't mind," I said. I grabbed a loaf of bread and opened it. "What kind of sandwiches should I make?"

"There's some ham in the refrigerator—"

"Gib!" I yelled. "You aren't going back to sleep, are you?"

"Shh!" my mother said. "Your dad's still asleep. Or *was*, anyway . . ." She ran her hand over my hair. "Don't be all day out at the airfield, all right? I don't want the sun cooking you and your brother till you're well done." Gib and I both have red-blond hair, and ever since my mother read an article in *The Stacy's Corners News* about sunburn she's convinced we cook faster than regular-headed people.

10

My mother went out to the living room and I started in on the lunch. I made the sandwiches, filled a thermos with iced tea, pulled a bag of Jay's potato chips out of the cupboard. I was organizing everything into a big grocery bag when I heard a knock on the kitchen-window screen.

"Hey there, Pokie," I heard Junior Hollinger say. "What are you doing?"

I looked at him looking at me through the screen. Junior was a year younger and two inches shorter than me. He'd wedged himself into the lilac tree so he could see into the kitchen.

I walked over to the window. "Didn't your mother ever tell you it's against the law to spy on people?"

"No," he said.

"I could have you arrested if I felt like it."

Junior shrugged. "Well? Do you feel like it?"

"No," I said. "Lucky for you. What happened to your head? It looks like an upside-down Fuller brush."

Junior patted his short, spiky hair. "Me and my pop just got back from Mr. Burgess' Barber Shop. They were having a two-for-one sale."

I went back to packing lunch. "You see 'The Amazing Colossal Man' on TV last night? I had to miss it because of Gib's graduation."

"Yeah, I seen it. . . . Hey, Pokie . . . you want to go with me out to Sunset Pool today? My ma says you can use her pass if you want to go—"

"I can't swim and you know it," I said.

"It's easy! I'll teach you—"

"Gib and I are going out to Mitchell and watch the planes land."

Junior shook his head. "I never knew anyone as crazy about planes as you are."

"Except Gib," I said.

"Yeah," he said. "Except Gib."

A half hour later Gib and I were out at Mitchell Field. Gib parked the car just inside the airport fence, right next to a sign that said:

DO NOT ENTER
NO TRESPASSING
VIOLATORS WILL BE PROSECUTED

I got out and climbed up on the roof of the car. Gib sat on the hood. He's tall—over six feet—and when he bends his long legs and sits on them he looks just like a human pretzel.

"Look behind you, Poke!" Gib yelled. "Piper Cherokee coming in for a landing!"

I watched as the small plane approached the runway. It looked like it was headed straight for our car. I watched as it came closer and closer, then *whoosh!* I was covered in the Cherokee's shadow and almost swallowed up in the roar of its engine.

Gib looked at me and grinned. "Only thing better than watching a Cherokee land would be flying one."

The little plane taxied down the runway and stopped, then two people got out: a young man and an older one. The older man had gray hair and reminded me of the janitor at our school.

"Look at the older man over there, Gib," I said. "Remember seeing him out here last summer? He's the one who gives the flying lessons."

Gib squinted in the sun. "Wonder how much he charges."

"Want me to go ask him?"

"What? Nah . . . I couldn't afford it anyway. I have to save all my money; I've got college coming up this fall."

"Yeah," I said. "I forgot."

I *had* forgotten. We watched the planes take off and land, but this college business was stuck in my head.

"Gib? Won't you be homesick? Going away to college in Missouri?"

"Hell, no," he said. "I've been looking forward to college for a long time. I can't wait to get there."

"Oh. I would think you'd be homesick."

We watched the pilot take student after student up for their lessons. I waved to the pilot each time he climbed out of the airplane and each time he waved back.

Gib was disgusted. "Good grief, Poke . . . you

13

want that guy to think you're some hick who's never even seen an airplane?"

"He doesn't think that," I said. "He just thinks I'm someone who likes flying."

We sat next to the car in a patch of shade to eat our lunch. While I was taking a big swallow of tea I noticed the pilot across the airfield; he was walking over to us.

"Gib . . . look who's coming—"

Gib looked up. "Shoot . . . he's going to make us leave because I'm parked here—"

"Hello there," the pilot said. "Since we're on a hand-waving basis, I thought I'd come over and introduce myself. I'm Hank Jellies."

I jumped up and shook his hand. "I'm Pokie and this is my brother, Gib. Gib's going to be a pilot someday."

Hank Jellies looked at Gib and smiled. "That right?"

"Well, I hope to," Gib said. "Someday."

"You're the one who gives the flying lessons, aren't you?" I asked. "How much does a lesson cost?"

"An introductory lesson's seventy-five dollars," Hank Jellies said. "You two like to take a look inside the Cherokee?"

"*Really?*" I said. "Come on, Gib!"

Gib stood up. "Thanks, Mr. Jellies. That's real nice of you." It was hard not to laugh: Gib was trying to sound grown-up and cool, but I knew he was just as excited as I was.

We followed Hank Jellies across the airfield to the Cherokee. He opened the door and we peeked inside. "Think you'd like to fly a plane like this someday?"

"I sure would," Gib said. "How about *you*, Poke? You should think about flying lessons, too; you're as crazy about planes as I am—"

"Me?" In the back of my head I'd always pictured Gib as the pilot, not me. Gib, flying low and circling twice. Twice, so I'd know it was him.

"Lots of lady pilots nowadays," Hank Jellies said. He checked his watch. "Oops . . . I better go collect my next student. You two want to sit in the plane till I get back?"

"Wow!" I said.

Hank Jellies laughed and walked around the plane and opened the other door. "Just don't take off, okay? The F.A.A. wouldn't like it."

Gib and I climbed into the Piper Cherokee.

"Look, Poke, here on the instrument panel— there's the altimeter . . . and you know what this is? This is the tachometer—"

"Shoot, I know what most of these things are," I said. "This is the airspeed indicator, right?"

"Yep . . ."

"Gib? You really think I could be a pilot?"

"You'd be a great pilot. Don't forget, you make the best paper airplanes."

I smiled. I thought about Gib and me getting

our pilot's licenses and running a brother-sister airport. I decided I could fly the northern route of the country, and Gib could fly the southern route because that way he wouldn't have to see the snow he hates to shovel.

"This is really something, isn't it?" Gib asked.

"Yeah," I said. I leaned back in my seat. "It really is."

That was the first time I'd ever sat in the cockpit of a plane.

3

"I tell you about meeting that pilot out at Mitchell Field?" I asked Junior. We'd just come out of Woolworth's and we were sharing a cherry Sno-Cone.

"Yeah, Pokie, yeah. You told me all about meeting him and how you want to be a pilot someday."

I frowned. "Well, I listen to all *your* stories, you know."

"I know. Maybe you'll give me a free ride when you're a pilot, huh?"

"Sure. You can come on up to the cockpit and I'll let you drive for a while."

"Look, Pokie . . ." Junior pointed to a red, white, and blue poster taped to Woolworth's window:

Stacy's Corners
Annual Carnival
Rides!
Games!
Fun for the whole family!
June 20–27

"You going?" Junior asked.

"Course I'm going."

"My ma said she'd drop me off right after dinner so I can get there early and ride the Ferris wheel all night. You think they'll put my picture in the paper if I ride the Ferris wheel all night?"

"Every year you swear you're gonna ride the Ferris wheel all night and you never do."

Junior took a big bite of the Sno-Cone. "I think they probably would," he said, "put my picture in the paper. I might even get a call from the TV station and go on down there and get interviewed."

"If they put your picture in the paper, it'll be because you're a twelve-year-old boy who wears lipstick."

"Lipstick!"

"Take a look at yourself in the window."

Junior squinted at his reflection. His lips were bright red from the Sno-Cone.

"I suppose you think this is funny," he said.

I gave him a pat on the back. "Yeah," I said. "Pretty funny."

That night Gib and I drove downtown to the carnival. As we headed down Pennsylvania, I could just barely see the outline of the Ferris-wheel lights over the tops of the trees.

"I'm going to win me a watch this year," I said. "Last year they had a lady's watch at the ring toss, but I ran out of money for the hoops."

"Poke, why don't you just save up your money and buy a watch? Probably'd be cheaper than wasting all your money on the ring toss—"

"I don't want to buy a watch, Gib. I want to win one."

"Remember that shrunken head I used to have hanging up in my room? I won that at the ring toss one year."

"Yeah, I remember that. . . . Hey, where do you think the carnival found a shrunken head? In a jungle somewhere?"

"Poke, it wasn't a real shrunken head. It was rubber. You don't think they'd sell a real shrunken head in Stacy's Corners, do you?"

"I don't know," I said. "Shoot . . . I always thought it was real. . . ."

Gib bought himself a box of popcorn and me a cotton candy. We watched the cotton-candy lady spin a fluffy pink web onto a paper cone. She handed it to me and I took a big bite out of it and let it melt on my tongue.

"Hey, Pokie!" I heard Junior Hollinger yell. He ran over to us, carrying a stuffed panda bear almost half his size. "Hi there, Gib. Hey, Pokie, you want this?"

"Really?"

Junior pushed the panda into my arms. "I won him by knocking over three milk bottles with a baseball. I was trying to win one of those radio-controlled airplanes for you, but I got this instead."

"Thanks."

"I understand you're out to set some sort of record on the Ferris wheel tonight, huh, Junior?" Gib said.

"Yeah. You think they'll put my picture in the paper if I stay on the Ferris wheel all night, Gib?"

"Only one way to find out. Come on."

We walked over to the Ferris-wheel booth and bought tickets. As soon as the Ferris-wheel man locked Gib, me, the panda, and Junior into our seat, Junior started breathing in quick, raspy breaths.

"I've changed my mind," he said in a loud voice. "Let me out of here!"

"Pipe down!" I said. "What's the matter with you? I thought you wanted your picture in the paper—"

The Ferris-wheel man sighed and came over and unlocked the bar across us, and Junior jumped out.

"I just remembered an article I read about a girl who fell off a Ferris wheel in Iowa," Junior said. "They found her the next day in Texas or someplace."

The wheel started moving. I looked at Gib.

"He does this every single year," I said. "I swear . . . I don't know what I'm going to do with that boy. . . ."

Up we went. We stopped at the top of the wheel and the seat rocked a little.

"Look how clear the sky is, Poke . . . all the stars are out."

I looked around. There was a spectacular night view of town; white squares of light from store windows dotted the landscape. We could see the orange-and-yellow top of the merry-go-round canopy and the roller-coaster lights as they flashed by below us.

"It's like having our own private kingdom to look down on," I said.

"Queen Pokie the First," Gib said, and I laughed.

"Hey, Gib . . . how come you nicknamed me Pokie?"

"You've heard that story a million times."

"Tell me again," I said. "Come on . . . you're not going anywhere. . . ."

"All right," Gib said. "Okay . . . let's see . . . when Mom and Dad brought you home from the hospital they told me your name was Alwilda, but I

21

just couldn't remember it—"

"And you wanted them to take me back to the hospital, right?"

"Sure," Gib said, "and trade you in for a baby with an easier name to remember . . . but they kept you, unfortunately—"

I socked Gib on the arm.

"And when you started to crawl you poked along, so I guess that's when I started calling you Pokie—"

"If I didn't have an older brother, I'd be walking around this earth answering to the name Alwilda. Lord!"

Gib laughed. "Bet there'll come a day when you decide to use your real name. I just can't picture the name 'Pokie' on a driver's license or a college diploma—"

"You'll see," I said.

The wheel started moving. We skimmed by Junior a couple of times; from what I could tell he was stuffing his face with hot dogs. When we got back to earth and stopped, the Ferris-wheel man grabbed our seat and steadied it while we hopped off.

"Hey, Junior," I said. "You notice that Gib and I didn't fall off the wheel and end up in Texas or someplace?"

"Yeah, I noticed," Junior said. "Guess what. I decided to set the world's record for hot-dog eating."

"Maybe you'll get your picture in the paper after all," Gib said. "I'm gonna go get myself one of those hot dogs, Poke. You want one?"

"Nah, I'm not hungry. You guys go ahead; I'll meet you at the ring toss."

The ring-toss booth had prizes set up on blocks of wood, prizes you had to throw a hoop over to win. I saw a rubber shrunken head like the one Gib had once owned, and other things, like a yo-yo, a compass, a Fred Flintstone pencil box, a harmonica, and some plastic vomit. The expensive things were set up in the back of the booth: a transistor radio, a set of binoculars, a fancy fountain pen, and the lady's watch I wanted.

The man at the counter held up three hoops. "Three for a dollar. Want to give it a try?"

I pulled out a dollar and handed it to him. "I want to win that lady's watch in the back there."

The first two hoops I threw bounced off the wooden block the watch sat on; the third teetered over the edge of the block, then fell to the ground.

"Give me another three," I said.

I ended up spending five dollars at the ring-toss booth. I noticed Gib after I threw the last hoop and missed; he was finishing up his hot dog and watching me with a critical eye.

"How much did you spend?" he asked.

"Five dollars."

Gib looked at the man behind the counter. "Let

23

me see those hoops."

The man tilted his head sideways. "You'll have to pay for them, son."

"The expensive things look like they're set up on bigger blocks. There's no way those hoops'll slide over them—"

The ring-toss man frowned. "Look . . . I don't want to get into an argument with you, son. Suppose you just go on your way now—"

I tugged on Gib's sleeve. "C'mon, Gib . . . it's not important—"

Gib leaned his elbows on the counter. "My sister's paid you five dollars for a chance to win that lady's watch—it'd be real nice if you gave her a fair shot at it." Gib didn't raise his voice. He didn't have to: He looked plenty mad. The ring-toss man cleared his throat a couple of times. He grabbed the lady's watch off the block and put it down in front of me.

"No," Gib said. "She'll win it on her own."

The man turned a vivid shade of purple. He knocked the harmonica off its wooden block, set the watch on it, and slapped three hoops down in front of me.

"Go ahead, Poke," Gib said. "You can do it."

I held my breath as I tossed the hoop. It slipped neatly over the watch and settled at the bottom of the block. The ring-toss man grabbed the watch and threw it to me.

"Thanks!" I said.

"You don't have to thank him, Poke," Gib said. "You won it fair and square."

The watch sparkled on my wrist. I held it up so Gib could see the time. "I'll always remember how you helped me get it," I said. "Every time I look at it."

"What are brothers for?" Gib said. He mussed my hair up by scrubbing his fingers through it.

"Hey, you're giving me static electricity!"

"I kind of like your hair this way," Gib said. "You look just like the Bride of Frankenstein."

"Hardy-har-har," I said. I tossed the panda bear to him and tried to smooth my hair down.

"Pokie! Gib!" Junior Hollinger ran up to us. He had half a hot dog in his hand. "Gib, I'm up to six and a half hot dogs and there's not a newspaper photographer anywhere. What do you think I should do?"

Gib and I looked at each other. I guess we set each other off; we just couldn't stop laughing.

Junior frowned. "You guys shouldn't laugh at someone who has over six hot dogs in his stomach."

"Come on, Junior," Gib said. "We'll give you a ride home. Maybe next year you can call ahead and make sure there are some newspaper people here."

"Well," Junior said. "All right. I *am* getting a little sick of hot dogs. . . ."

———

On the way home I showed Junior my watch and told him about Gib and the ring-toss man.

"No kidding, Gib? I seen that guy earlier. He looked mean. Did you really talk back to him?"

"He really did," I said. "The man turned purple and I got scared, but Gib wasn't. He stood right up to him."

"Man!" Junior said. "You're lucky you have an older brother, Pokie, you know it?"

I noticed Gib smiling a little.

"Yeah," I said. "I know it."

4

"You're swinging too low, Pokie," Gib said. I had just swung the bat and missed a pitch from Junior Hollinger. Gib stood at the back door shaking his head. "Try it again."

Junior threw the ball.

I swung the bat.

The ball flew over my shoulder.

"This is hopeless!" Junior said. "I been doing this all morning and she hasn't hit it once!"

Gib tossed the ball to Junior. "Pokie, you're holding the bat all wrong. . . ." He stood behind me and held his hands over mine. "Okay, Junior, go ahead."

Junior pitched the ball. Gib held on to my

hands tight and swung the bat with me. *CRACK!* The ball sailed clear over the backyard fence. The impact of the ball on the bat sent vibrations down my arms.

Junior was impressed. "Wow! Think you could teach me to hit like that, Gib?"

"Sure."

My mother appeared at the back door. "Junior Hollinger? Your mom just called. She wants you to come home for lunch—"

"What's she making?" Junior asked.

My mother looked at him. "Fried eye of newt and electric eels."

Junior grinned. "Your ma's funny, Pokie. I'll see you later."

"You want to do something after lunch?" I asked.

"Can't," he said. "I have a dentist appointment. I might be getting braces on my teeth."

"Your teeth don't look so crooked to me—"

"Dentist says they don't mesh right or something. 'Bye!"

"'Bye . . ."

Junior cut through our driveway, stepping on every crack he came to.

"He's always stepping on those cracks," I said. "He swears it gives his mother a backache."

"I think Junior's more likely to give her a headache, don't you?" my mother said. "Listen, you two can get your own lunch, can't you? I have to go over to Kate's for a little while."

Kate, our grandmother, lived in the house next to ours.

"You going over to Kate's to make cookies or something?" I asked, and my mother smiled.

"We have some typing to do for the League of Women Voters. Be good now, you hear?"

"There's nothing to do," I told Gib after lunch. "I was going to talk Junior into going to the movies, but he's off getting his teeth inspected."

"The movies!" Gib said. "You don't want to waste a beautiful day like this going to the *movies*, do you?"

"Well, sure I do. They're showing *The Attack of the Fifty-Foot Woman*."

"Want to go swimming?"

"Swimming . . . can't you think of something else to do?"

"You're thirteen, Poke. About time you learned to swim, isn't it?"

"I don't see what's so important about swimming. I could name a hundred famous people who can't swim."

"Well, I'm going," Gib said. "You want to come along or are you gonna stay home with nothing to do but make a list of your hundred famous people who can't swim?"

"I guess I'll come," I said. "But I'm not going in the deep end."

There was hardly any traffic on the road to Sunset Pool.

"Hey, Gib," I said, "how about letting me drive a little?"

"*What?* Are you crazy?"

"Just a couple miles. Come on, Gib. Nothing'll happen. Hell, we're practically the only car on the road right now—"

"The state of Illinois says you have to wait till you're sixteen to drive and that's fine by me."

"Seems to me I remember a time you took Kate's old Chevrolet for a little spin. You couldn't have been more than ten at the time."

Gib shook his head. "I didn't go for a 'spin,' Poke. They were spraying the trees on our street for Dutch elm disease, and I was just trying to get Kate's car out of the way, that's all."

"Ha!" I said. "Dutch elm disease . . ."

"Maybe I'll let you drive on the way home. If you let me teach you how to swim."

"That's not fair!" I said. "If I get drowned, I won't even be *going* home!"

"Poke, you won't be scared of the deep end once you know how to swim—"

"Forget it! The deal's off! I don't care if you *won't* let me drive the car; I'm not going in the deep end."

"Have it your own way," Gib said.

At the pool Gib and I went our separate ways into the men's and women's changing rooms. I pulled on my swimsuit, took my towel, and went out to the pool. I noticed Gib up on the high diving board. He walked to the edge, jumped, and did a graceful dive.

"Show-off," I mumbled. I sat down and dangled my legs in the water and watched Gib swim over to me.

"You coming in?" he said.

"Yeah, I'm coming in. I'm gonna get in the shallow end just as soon as you swim away."

Gib smiled wickedly. "You afraid I might pull you in?"

"Gib, cut it out now—"

"C'mon in, Poke." He grabbed my wrist and *splash!* I was in the water.

"I swear, I'm gonna kill you!" I said.

Gib put his arms around me and held me up so the water was about waist high. "See? It's not all that deep here—"

"Don't let go of me!"

"I'm not going to let go of you . . . here . . . hang on to the edge of the pool and kick—"

"What for?!"

"It's how you learn to swim. Come on now, Poke . . . you don't want to go through the rest of your life not knowing how to swim—"

I shook some wet hair out of my eyes. "Promise you'll catch me if I start to sink."

"I promise. Grab the edge of the pool."

I held on to the edge of the pool and kicked for a minute, then I kicked with Gib holding on to my hands. When I was able to float and kick at the same time, Gib let go of me and I was swimming! I swam to the edge of the pool and back to Gib again. He picked me up and whirled me around and we both sank, but I held my breath and popped right out of the water. So did Gib.

"I knew you could do it, Poke—"

"Wait'll I show Junior—hey, Gib, let's go over to the diving board. You could swim around below me and catch me after I jump off."

He laughed. "I don't think you're exactly ready for the diving board yet. You have to practice your swimming a lot before you try that." He dunked me in the pool and I splashed water in his face.

"How come you wanted me to learn how to swim, Gib?"

"I don't know," Gib said. "You can do practically everything else . . . just didn't seem right you couldn't swim—"

"You didn't forget our deal, did you?"

"No," Gib said. "I didn't forget."

As soon as Gib pulled away from the traffic at the parking lot he slowed the car to a stop. "I can't believe I'm doing this," he said. "All right now, listen. I don't want you going over ten miles an hour, understand?"

"Yeah, ten miles an hour! I promise!"

"And whatever you do, don't tell Mom and Dad—"

"You think I'm crazy?"

Gib pushed himself up out of the seat and I scrunched under him to the driver's side.

"Don't forget your seat belt," I said. "And for God's sake, quit looking so worried!"

"I've got my freshman year at college coming up, you know," Gib said. "I'd like to live to enjoy it."

"Shoot, there's nothing to be scared of." I put the car in drive and eased forward. "I've been watching people drive cars my whole life."

"Look out now . . . keep your eyes on the road . . ."

I knew what I was doing: I drove slowly, checked for traffic, kept the car going steady and in the right lane. It was a beautiful day. Trees lined both sides of the road and formed a lush arc that we drove under; the leaf shadows played on the pavement.

Gib let me drive all the way home. As I pulled into our driveway I noticed our grandmother Kate watching us. She stood by her rosebushes, the garden hose in her hand. She looked so shocked to see me behind the wheel of the car that she ended up watering her sidewalk instead of the roses.

Gib and I looked at each other, then at Kate.

Kate redirected the water to her roses and smiled a little.

"Don't worry. I didn't see a thing," she said. "Not a thing."

5

Junior knocked on the screen door and flashed me a metal smile.

"Hey there, Pokie."

"You got 'em!" I said. I went out and put my hands on his shoulders and took a good look at his braces. "Neat!"

"You really think so? I can't stand me in the mirror anymore."

"They make you look very sophisticated."

"Thanks, Pokie. You want to come help me? I'm fixing up my treehouse—"

"That rickety old thing?" I said. "Thought you gave up on it last year—"

"It's not so rickety. I think it just needs a few more nails in it is all."

Gib opened the screen door. "You get your braces, Junior?"

"What do you think, Gib? Do my teeth look any straighter yet?"

"Let me see," Gib said. He bent down and looked at Junior's teeth. "You know, I think they *do* look a little straighter."

Gib gave Junior a pat on the back and walked over to our car. Junior and I followed him.

"Where are you going?" I asked. "Can we come, too?"

"I don't think so, Poke. I'm going to work."

"Work! Since when?"

"Since this morning when I got a job at Dog 'N' Suds."

"Hey, the Dog 'N' Suds!" Junior said. "You think you could get Pokie and me some free root beers and cheese dogs?"

Gib smiled. "We'll see. . . ."

"You never told me you were getting a job," I said. "What do you want to do that for?"

"I need the money, Poke."

"You saving up for that introductory flying lesson out at Mitchell?"

"Nope. College." He got in the car and pulled the door shut. "I've got to help Mom and Dad all I can; my tuition's costing them a fortune."

"Oh . . ."

"See you later. . . ."

We watched him drive away.

"You know something, Pokie?" Junior said. "Gib's turning into a grown-up."

I shrugged. "Just 'cause he's going to cook hot dogs for a living doesn't mean he's a grown-up."

"I don't mean anything about hot dogs."

"I know," I said, but it bothered me a little. Gib turning into a grown-up meant Gib going off to college and not being around anymore. "Hey, Junior . . . you ever think about growing up and leaving home and stuff like that?"

Junior shook his head. "No," he said, "I don't weigh my brains down with stuff like that."

We spent the rest of the afternoon trying to repair Junior's treehouse. It was more of a platform than anything else—and a pretty dilapidated one at that. We banged about sixty million nails into the wooden planks before my mother stopped us.

"Pokie!" She stood the seven or eight feet below us with her hands on her hips. "What all are you and Junior doing up there?"

"Fixing Junior's treehouse."

"I don't want you up on that thing; you'll fall and break your neck."

"I'm not going to fall," I said.

"I want you down from there right now. And Junior Hollinger? Do you think your mother would be very happy if she knew you were up on that broken-down old platform?"

Junior thought a second. "Well . . . she might be a *little* nervous."

"I'd say she'd be a *lot* nervous. Now, come on down here, both of you."

This was the way our neighborhood worked: A mother didn't tell someone else's child what to do unless there was a potential broken neck involved.

I climbed carefully down the ladder. Junior followed. My mother looked at me. "I'm going over to Kate's for a bit; we're finishing up some work for the League. You two find something else to do, okay?"

"Like what?" Junior asked.

"How about baseball?" my mother said, and Junior made this ugly kind of snorting noise.

"The only time Pokie can ever hit the ball is when Gib helps her."

"Well, find something safe to do," my mother said. "I can't be typing a report if I'm worried about you. See you later."

"'Bye," I said.

As soon as my mother was safely out of sight Junior and I climbed back up to the treehouse.

We stood on the platform and admired the work we'd done.

"Guess what, Pokie," Junior said. "We only have two nails left."

"Well, we can't hammer 'em in; my mother'd hear and come back and really give it to us."

"Give what to us?"

"It! You know what 'it' means."

"Oh, yeah," Junior said.

"I don't think your treehouse needs more nails anyway," I said. "I think it needs decorating. A rug and a chair, maybe."

"Pokie, you think we could have a little kitchen up here? If we had a refrigerator and a stove up here we could cook."

I looked at him. "How would we get a refrigerator and a stove up here? Your whole problem is you don't think things through enough."

"Pokie!" I heard Gib say. I peeked over the edge of the platform. "What the hell are you doing up there? You trying to kill yourself?"

"No, I'm not trying to *kill* myself," I said. "Sometimes you treat me like I don't have a brain in my head. How come you're home, anyway? I thought you were down at Dog 'N' Suds making a million dollars for college."

"They just trained me today," Gib said. He held up a red-and-white-striped bag. "Brought you and Junior some cheese dogs."

"Cheese dogs!" Junior said. "We'll be right down. Hurry up, Pokie."

I hurried. I caught my foot on a board we hadn't been able to nail down. I made a wild grab for the edge of the platform but couldn't hang on to it. I tumbled to the ground with an awful thud and landed on my back.

Junior looked down. "Pokie! Are you murdered?"

"No, I'm not murdered . . . I just got skinned up is all."

Gib had sent the bag of cheese dogs flying. He knelt down and put his hand on my head. "Poke?"

"Don't tell Mom, Gib. Promise. She'll pitch a fit. Promise you won't tell."

Gib bit his lip. He looked me over, held up my hand. "You've got a monster splinter in your hand here—"

"Promise."

"All right. All right, I promise. We'll have to get you cleaned up before she comes back. . . . Can you stand up?"

He helped me to my feet. Junior came slinking down the ladder. He looked very worried.

"You must be hurt bad," he said. "You almost never cry unless you hurt bad."

"I'm not crying!" I said. "My eyes are wet from falling!"

"Oh."

Gib took me by the shoulders. "She'll be okay, Junior. . . . You better stay out of that treehouse yourself."

Junior nodded and bit on his knuckles. Gib took me home, up to the bathroom. He washed and bandaged up my knee, then he got some tweezers to take out the splinter. Junior was someone I had to be brave in front of, but I could be myself with Gib. He held my hand and worked on it, and I started crying for real.

"I'm sorry, Poke, but it's a nasty splinter—"

"It's not that. Mom'll kill me if she finds out. She told me to stay out of that treehouse just five minutes before I fell."

"She's not going to find out," Gib said. "Hell, even if she did she wouldn't kill you. Know why? Because I was born first and got her used to stuff like this."

I wiped my eyes on my sleeve. "Yeah?"

"Sure. I've done a million things worse than fall out of a treehouse without permission."

I laughed. Gib was always good at making me see the funny side. "Gib? What'll I do when you're at college? I'm really going to miss you. . . ."

Gib sprayed my finger with some Bactine. "I'm going to miss you, too . . . but I'll be home for holidays . . . and summers . . ."

"But it won't be the same. It won't be the same as having you around all the time."

41

"No," he said. He wrapped a bandage around my finger. "It won't be the same."

That night was the first time I had my "tree-house dream," as I later came to call it: I felt myself tripping off the edge of the platform and tumbling wildly over and over. I hit the ground and landed on my back, but this time Gib wasn't there beside me. Gib was gone. I woke with a start. I climbed out of bed and went and got a slurp of water from the bathroom faucet, but I just couldn't shake that spooky "night-mare" feeling. Gib's door was open; his light was on. I walked down the hall and stood in the doorway.

"Gib?"

He was sitting at his desk. He looked up from the book he was reading. "Poke . . . what are you doing up?"

"I had a dream I was falling out of the tree-house. I couldn't find you anywhere. . . ."

"Come on." He picked up his book and walked me back to my room. I got into bed and he pulled the covers up. "I'll read to you till you're asleep, okay?"

I nodded, and he turned on the little reading lamp by my bed.

"You'll like this book; it's all about jets. I was just reading about the 727. . . ."

I listened as he read about the 727 in a low voice. I didn't dream about falling again. Instead I was flying, piloting my own 727, with Gib right beside me.

6

"You did not drive," Junior said.

"I most certainly did," I said. "Didn't I, Gib?"

"What? Yeah," Gib said. "She did. But just a little."

I was sitting at the picnic table, putting together a model of a Piper Cherokee. Gib was lying in the lounge chair, working on his tan, and Junior sat next to me, my uninvited aviation advisor.

"You got the wings crooked," Junior said.

"I know it," I said. "I'm not done yet." I straightened the wings and held them steady while the glue dried. "Anyway, Gib says I'm a natural-born driver. Says I drive better than most of the grownups on the road."

Gib sighed. "Pokie . . ."

"Well, you sort of said it." I took the plane over to Gib and showed it to him.

"Pretty slick," Gib said. He held the plane up and spun the little propeller. "Bet you didn't even need the directions, did you?"

"Nope. Looks just like Hank Jellies' plane, doesn't it? You think we could take it out to Mitchell and show it to him?"

"Sure. Let's go on out there," Gib said. "Junior? You want to come with us and watch the planes land?"

"Nah . . . I'm going to open up a lemonade stand this afternoon and make two hundred dollars."

"Two hundred dollars!" I said.

"Yeah, I got it all figured out, Pokie. I'm gonna charge a dollar a glass. Now all I need is two hundred people."

"Good luck," I said. "You'll need it!"

I noticed the sky darkening as we drove to Mitchell. The air seemed different. Pressurized. Like it was building up to something.

"We're in for a storm," I said, and Gib nodded. "Hey, Gib . . . you think they have a cyclone cellar at your college? You better find out. They have tornadoes in Missouri, you know."

"They have tornadoes right here in Illinois, Poke."

"Not as bad as Missouri," I said. "Remember

45

The Wizard of Oz."

"That was Kansas!" Gib said. "I don't think you have to worry about a tornado picking up the University of Missouri and setting it down on some witch, do you?"

I started laughing. "Well, you never know what's going to happen, Gib. You better watch out for those flying monkeys now."

"The monkeys scared *you*, not me," Gib said. "The Tin Man's the one who gave *me* nightmares."

We were into a full-scale thunderstorm by the time we reached Mitchell. Great sheets of rain hit the windshield and I could see zigzag flashes of lightning against the dark sky.

"*Look* at this!" Gib said. He stopped the car next to the airfield fence. "We sure as hell aren't gonna see any planes take off today."

"Think we should start home?"

"Not till it lets up. Come on. Let's get into the airport office; I don't want to be stuck in the car if a twister *does* hit."

I tucked the little Cherokee plane under my arm. Gib and I were soaked as soon as we stepped out of the car; we made a mad dash against the wind to get to the airport office. Gib slammed the doors shut behind us and we tried to shake off some of the wetness.

"Mr. Jellies?" Gib called. "Anyone here?"

"Shoot, we made the trip all the way out here for nothing," I said. I set the Cherokee down on the counter and looked around. There was a sign on the wall:

MITCHELL AIRPORT
Introductory Flying Lesson
Piper Cherokee
One hour—$75.00
Hank Jellies, pilot

Gib spun a rack of postcards around and looked at them. I walked over to a cluttered desk and studied some picture frames hung over it; they were filled with medals of some kind.

"Gib, look at these. . . ."

Gib walked over and looked at the medals. "These are army medals, Poke. They must be Hank Jellies'. See this little one shaped like a caterpillar? Means he's a member of the caterpillar club. He had to parachute out of his plane to get that. . . . Maybe his plane was shot down during the war. . . . This looks like him in the picture here."

There was a cracked, yellowed newspaper clipping in a frame on the desk. The picture showed a young Hank Jellies in an army uniform standing next to an A-20. The headline said: "World War II Hero Comes Home."

I picked up a brown leather jacket hanging on the back of the desk chair. Silver pilot's wings

47

were pinned on it.

"Hey, Gib, look . . . a flying jacket like pilots wear in those old movies. Try it on."

"What? I'm not gonna try it on—"

"Come on. Look. It even has pilot's wings on it. Put it on and pretend you're a famous World War II pilot."

Gib took the jacket from me and looked at it for a second. "I'm too old for make-believe," he said.

"No, you're not. Come on. You know you're dying to put it on."

He shook his head. "Oh, what the hell . . ." He slipped the jacket on. He looked down and traced the silver wings with one finger.

"You look just like a real pilot."

Gib put his hands in the jacket pockets. He pulled out a pair of aviator sunglasses.

"Wow! Put 'em on, Gib. Let's see how you look—"

Gib slid the sunglasses on.

"All you need now is a plane," I said.

"And a pilot's license."

"You'll get one someday."

"You will too, Poke. But until then . . ." He took off the jacket and draped it over my shoulders. I looked down at the pilot's wings. Gib may have been reluctant to play make-believe, but not me. I grabbed the Cherokee model off the counter and ran across the office.

48

"Piper Cherokee requesting permission to take off," I said.

Gib laughed. "Piper Cherokee, you're cleared for takeoff, but please make sure your rubber band is wound and your glue has dried."

Gib was right; he was pretty old to be playing make-believe and I guess I was, too, but we kept it up until the rain stopped and the sky lightened. Before we left I hung the jacket on the chair. I left the little Cherokee plane on the desk, right next to Hank Jellies' faded newspaper clipping.

"Don't you want to leave him a note?" Gib asked. "How's he gonna know who left it?"

"He's not," I said, "but it's more fun this way. Like Santa Claus or something."

Gib grinned. "Come on. Let's go home."

I always remember that afternoon, because it was the last time Gib and I had the chance to be just plain silly.

To play.

It was the last time we were really kids.

7

I sat behind the wheel of the car. Junior sat beside me, biting his thumbnail.

"Pokie, you sure we should be doing this?" he asked. "What if we get caught?"

"We're not going to get caught," I said. "Kate and my mother are out shopping and Gib's busy sorting out all the junk he's taking to college."

"You promise you'll just drive down to the corner and back?"

"I promise!" I said. "Lord, some people have no sense of adventure." I put the car in reverse and backed out of the driveway.

"There's a car coming! You better be careful—"

"I see it. Quit being such a worrywart." I drove

the car to the corner and stopped at the stop sign. "See? Nothing to it."

"Okay, Pokie, okay. I believe you. You can drive. Now just turn the car around—"

"I'll make a U-turn like Gib does when he forgets something and has to go back home."

I checked to make sure no traffic was coming, then I turned the wheel all the way to the left and stepped on the accelerator. Junior clamped his hands over his eyes.

"There's nothing to be scared of," I said. "See? We're almost home."

I turned too soon. Instead of going into the driveway, the car bumped up over the curb and rolled right into a tree. There was a terrific *crunch*.

Junior looked at me, his eyes huge. "Man, are you in *trouble!* I'm getting out of here!" He jumped out of the car and ran off. "Thanks for the ride!"

"Junior, don't leave me!" I yelled.

Gib leaned out his bedroom window. "Holy God! What *happened*?" He disappeared. I knew he was on his way downstairs so I scrambled out of the car and raced over to Junior's yard. Junior was spinning around on his tire swing.

"Hey there," I said.

"You almost just got me killed and all you can say is 'Hey there'?"

"I didn't almost kill you," I said.

"You aren't supposed to leave the scene of an accident, Pokie."

"That's only if you run over someone!"

"I think it's against the law to hit-and-run a tree, isn't it?"

"I just bumped it is all!"

"Sounded like you took the whole front fender off. I read in one of those newspapers at the supermarket checkout line one time that trees cry when they're cut down. Only it's not tears; it's sap. You think that tree felt anything when you ran into it, Pokie?"

"Lord, I'm sorry I even came *over* here—"

"Pokie!" I heard Gib yell.

"So that's why you're here," Junior said. "You're hiding from Gib, huh?"

"I'm not hiding from him!" I said. "I just don't want him to find me."

"Get under the porch steps. He won't find you there."

I crawled under the steps. My face went right through a spiderweb.

"Pokie!" Gib hollered. "You over here?" I peeked through some cracks in the step and watched Gib walk over to Junior. "You seen Pokie, Junior?"

"Nope," Junior said. He twisted the swing tight, let go of it, and spun with his head bent way back. "I love making myself dizzy, don't you, Gib?"

"No," Gib said. "But it explains a few things about *you.*"

"I think I saw Pokie under some porch on Hawthorne Street," Junior said. "She's not over here anywhere."

Shut up, you little weasel, I thought.

"Junior . . . didn't I see you jump out of our car a few minutes ago? Right after it hit the tree?"

"I didn't do it, Gib! Honest!"

"Oh, I know," Gib said. He walked over to the steps and sat down. I could see the backs of his legs through the cracks. I tried to quiet my breathing. "You know, there's this big dent in the front fender. . . . I think it can probably be pounded out, though. . . ."

"I don't know *where* Pokie is, Gib. I bet you wouldn't find her even if you searched the whole yard."

Junior, you moron! I thought.

"I know Pokie'd never take the car out on her own"—I was sure I felt my heart stop—"but if you see her," Gib said, "tell her I'm taking the car down to the garage before Mom and Dad get home, okay?"

"Okay," Junior said in a quiet voice. "I'll tell her."

This was just too much for me. I crawled out from under the porch. "Gib?"

"Junior, you better tell your mother to call the exterminator," Gib said. "Looks like you've got some sort of varmint living under your porch."

Junior squealed. He sounded like a cross between a hyena and a drunken goat. "Hey, Pokie, you hear that? He called you a varmint!"

"I heard him!" I said. "I'm standing right here!" I looked at Gib. "You really going to have it fixed for me?"

"Depends," Gib said. His eyes were smiling. "You through with driving for a while?"

"I won't drive again till I'm sixteen," I said. "I promise."

"Let's go down to the garage."

I rubbed my eyes hard. "Thanks, Gib . . ."

He put his arm around my shoulders. "Come on, Poke . . . everything's okay now."

"I know. . . ."

"Junior," Gib said, "I wouldn't tell anyone about this afternoon if I were you."

"You don't have to worry, Gib. You know how good I am at keeping secrets."

Gib and I looked at each other.

"See you later, Junior," I said.

Junior was too busy twisting the tire-swing rope to answer. Gib and I started home.

The last time we looked back, Junior was spinning round and round, making himself dizzier than ever.

8

In late August a letter from the high school arrived for me. My grandmother and Junior Hollinger and I were all crowded in front of the TV set watching a Cubs game when my mother brought the mail in.

"Pokie, this just came for you," she said. I took the letter from her and forgot about it because I was all caught up in the game. Kate wore a Cubs baseball cap to bring the team luck, but it didn't help much that afternoon: They lost six to three.

"Maybe I should get a new cap," Kate said.

"Can I wear your hat for a while, Pokie's Gramma?" Junior asked. "I'll pretend I'm a Cub pitcher."

Kate put her cap on Junior's head. "There. You're an official member of the team."

Junior took a peek at the envelope in my hand. "Who's writing you from the high school?" he asked.

"I don't know." I ripped open the envelope. At the top of the paper inside was printed:

FRESHMAN ORIENTATION DAY

"This isn't fair," I said. "I don't want to give up a day of my vacation to go get oriented."

Kate looked at my mother. "Where does the time go? Gib's off to college soon and Pokie's going into high school."

"I can't believe you're old enough for high school," my mother said. "Seems like just yesterday I was taking you to kindergarten."

"You better be careful up there at that high school, Pokie," Junior said. "There are a million classrooms up there, and I heard that the teachers get mad if you get lost just a little."

I frowned. "Well, I won't get lost after I get oriented."

"How you going to get oriented around that huge place in just one day?"

"I don't know, but I will."

"I heard they got a teacher up there who was just released from a hospital for the criminally insane. She's teaching freshman English this year."

"Junior?" Kate said. "Something tells me you're going to be a writer when you grow up."

"I'm just telling you what I hear around town, Pokie's Gramma. This lady teacher went crazy from smelling Ditto-machine fumes." He looked at me sympathetically. "I'd be scared if I were you, Pokie. I'm glad I don't have to start high school yet."

"Well, unless you start getting better grades," I said, "you won't have to worry about high school at all."

He shrugged and pulled Kate's baseball cap low over his eyes. "Ha," he said.

Junior had said just enough to worry me. Enough so I got on my bike later that afternoon and pedaled down to Dog 'N' Suds. Gib was at the take-out window. He was doing a bunch of things at once: waiting on people, grilling hot dogs, making milk shakes.

"Hey there," Gib said. "What'll it be?"

"Root beer," I said. "Gib? I got a letter from the high school that says I have to go get oriented next week."

"Oh, yeah . . . Freshman Day. I remember that."

"Well, how am I going to learn my way around in just one day? Junior says the teachers get mad if you get lost even a little."

Gib set a big glass of root beer down in front of

me and stuck a straw in it. "Since when do you listen to Junior Hollinger? He doesn't know anything about high school; he's just starting the eighth grade."

"Well, I know, but . . . the only time I was up there at the high school was when you had your wind tunnel in the science fair, remember? I went looking for the girls' bathroom and I got lost in the boys' locker room."

Gib laughed. "Yeah, I remember. . . . I don't know who was more surprised. You, or the basketball team."

"This isn't funny," I said. "It's not, Gib. Junior says they've got a teacher up there who just got out of a hospital for the insane. She's teaching freshman English this year."

Gib didn't exactly laugh again, but it looked like he had tears in his eyes. "Pokie, you want me to take you by the high school when I'm through here? I'll show you around enough so you won't get lost."

"Really?"

"Why don't you put the backseat down in the car so we can get your bike in—I'll be finished here in a few minutes."

"Thanks, Gib. Thanks!"

The front doors of the high school were locked, but Gib knew about a side door that was always open, so we sneaked in that way.

"See?" he said. "What's so scary about this place?"

As we walked down the hall and peeked into some of the classrooms I had to agree with him. This was an old school; no fluorescent lights or vinyl flooring here. Sunlight spilled through big windows onto wooden floors. One of the classrooms had bright yellow letters tacked to the bulletin board that spelled out:

WELCOME, FRESHMEN

Gib showed me the cafeteria, the girls' bathrooms, and the drinking fountains.

"If you want cold water you'll have to use the refrigerated fountain upstairs," he said. "Come on . . . I want to show you where you'll probably have English class."

We went up to the second floor. Gib opened a classroom door and we walked inside.

"Well, Gib!" someone said, and we both jumped. "What are *you* doing here?"

The person talking to us was a pretty blond-haired woman who sat at the teacher's desk.

"Mrs. Turkel," Gib said. "Hi . . . um, this is my sister Po—I mean, Alwilda. She's going to be a freshman this year."

Mrs. Turkel smiled. She walked over to us and shook my hand. "Well, hi there, Alwilda. I believe you're in my third-period English class this semester."

"I am?"

She nodded. "You know, Gib was in my class when he was a freshman . . . that reminds me of something. Look over here." We followed her to the back of the room and looked at the desk she pointed to: The letters "GIB" were carved deep into the wood.

I ran my fingers over the letters.

"Your brother spent an afternoon in detention hall for that. Do you remember, Gib?"

Gib smiled, but he looked kind of embarrassed. "Well, I learned my lesson. I won't do it at college."

"That's right—you're off to college, aren't you? Well," Mrs. Turkel said, "I'm going to ask Alwilda here to keep me posted on how you're doing."

"Mrs. Turkel?" I said. "Could you please call me Pokie? It's my nickname. I just don't feel like an Alwilda most of the time."

She smiled. "See you next week then, Pokie."

"Well?" Gib said on the way home. "Does Mrs. Turkel look like she just got out of a hospital for the insane?"

"She was pretty nice," I said. "Junior got me scared for nothing."

"Pokie, you've got to remember something: 'Firsts' are always scary. Remember how scared you were when I taught you to ride your two-wheeler . . . or to swim?"

"Yeah, but Gib . . . you were never scared of anything, were you?"

"Sure. I'm scared now. Of college."

"Huh? But I thought you were all excited about that—"

"I am, Poke. But it's the first time I've ever gone to college so it's a little scary."

I had never thought about Gib being scared of anything. "It'll work out, Gib. You'll see. Once you get there and make a friend."

Gib nodded. "Good advice for you, too, Poke."

"Yeah," I said. "Yeah. I reckon it is."

9

The week before Gib left for college we went out to Mitchell Field one last time. I took along my Kodak and made him stand by a Cessna 152 so I could snap his picture.

"Make believe you just flew in from Italy or Peoria or someplace," I said.

"Pokie . . . just take the picture."

I took the picture.

"I'll send it to you at college," I said. "Look, Gib . . . that's Hank Jellies, isn't it?"

It was. Hank Jellies walked to his Piper Cherokee with a young man. Another student, I figured.

I waved wildly and Gib tried to grab my hands.

"Lord, Poke! You trying to mortify me? Can't you see he's with a student?"

"Hell, who knows when we'll be back here?" I said. "I just want to say good-bye to him."

Hank Jellies waved back and I took his picture as he walked over to us.

"I feel like a movie star, getting my picture taken," he said. "Haven't seen you two around lately."

"We were out here during that thunderstorm," I said. "But you weren't in the office—"

"I couldn't take students up during the storm so I canceled my lessons and went home till it blew over. . . ." He looked at me. "Funny thing . . . that was the day someone left a model airplane in the office. You didn't happen to see who left it, did you?"

"No," I said.

"A perfect replica of my Cherokee. I've got it front and center on my desk where everyone can see it."

I didn't say anything. Neither did Gib, but he gave me a nudge with his elbow.

"We wanted to come out here one last time before Gib leaves for college," I said. "He's going to the University of Missouri."

"College!" Hank Jellies said. "Won't be seeing you for a while then, hmm?"

"Not till next summer, I guess," Gib said.

"Wish I could stay and talk to you a bit, but I have a student waiting for me."

"Maybe next summer Gib and I'll come out and take a lesson or two."

"I'll look forward to that," he said. "Well, then." He shook Gib's hand. "Good luck at college now. You watch out for all those wild college girls."

Gib laughed. "I'll do my best."

Hank Jellies shook my hand. "So long till next summer, Future Lady Pilot."

"So long," I said.

We watched him walk across the field and climb into the plane.

"What'd he mean about wild college girls?" I asked.

"It's just a joke," Gib said.

"Oh."

"You think he knows I'm the one who left the Cherokee?"

"I think so."

I leaned against the car and watched Hank Jellies and his student take off in the Piper Cherokee. "Maybe someday that's us, huh?"

"Someday," Gib said. "Know what? I think we better get back. I have to finish packing my trunk so I can take it down to Railway Express."

I sat on the floor in Gib's room and handed him some of the winter clothes he had set aside to take to college.

"I think this pretty much does it," he said. "I just hope I can get it closed."

"Looks like you cleared out your whole room," I said. Gib's room just didn't look the same: The bookcase was emptied, his bedspread gone, his dresser cleared off, and his typewriter packed. The model airplanes were still there, though, hanging from the ceiling on their delicate wires.

"Aren't you taking any of your airplanes?" I asked. "Or your Piper Cub poster?"

"I don't think I'll have room for them," Gib said. "I'm just taking what I really need." Gib sat on the trunk and it squeezed shut.

"I guess you'll be pretty busy down there at college, huh?"

"Yeah, I guess so. . . ." He locked a padlock on the trunk. "You want any of my airplane stuff? You can take the Piper Cub poster if you want."

"Thanks," I said. I went over and pulled the thumbtacks out of the poster. "Gib? It won't be the same without you—"

"I'll be home before you know it."

"Not till Thanksgiving. . . . Think how long that is, Gib. It's so cold at Thanksgiving and right now it's blazing hot. A whole season has to pass before you're home again."

"It'll go fast," Gib said. "You'll see. Once you start school, time'll fly—"

"Who's going to help me with my homework if I get stuck? You know how bad Mom and Dad are at math—"

"Kate's the one who got me through algebra. She'll help you, too."

I started rolling up the poster. "Well, I just haven't ever not had you around."

I sounded pretty silly, but Gib didn't laugh. He walked over to me. "I think I know what you're trying to say."

"I'm going to miss you."

"I'm going to miss you, too."

"You're better than a brother, Gib. You're almost as good as a friend."

Now Gib laughed. He put his arms around me and gave me a monster hug. "Know what? I think you've been hanging around Junior too long."

My parents and Kate and Gib and I drove to O'Hare Airport early the next morning. Gib checked his suitcase and a small box in at the airline desk, then we began the long walk to the gate where he'd board his plane.

"What'd you have in that box you checked?" I asked.

"My clock radio and the airplane bank you made me."

"Yeah? You're taking the airplane bank?"

"Well, sure. How else can I make sure you don't raid it while I'm gone?"

"Shoot, I'm not the one who raids it," I said. "Didn't you ever notice all the I.O.U.'s are in Dad's handwriting?"

"Here we are," my father said. We walked into the waiting area and Gib walked over to the counter and showed the airline lady his ticket.

"I've made up my mind," my mother said. "I'm not going to cry."

"If *you* start crying that'll be it for me; I'll start," Kate said.

My father looked at me and winked. "Then Pokie and I'll start crying, and we'll make such a scene that the airport police will throw us out and it'll get on the six-o'clock news and we won't be able to show our faces anywhere—"

"Oh, you," my mother said. She gave him a gentle shove and he put his arm around her shoulders.

Gib walked over to us. "Well, I guess this is it. People are starting to board—"

"Wait a minute now," Kate said. She pulled a twenty-dollar bill out of her wallet. "A little mad money."

"Kate, I don't need any money; Dad's already slipped me some—"

"No arguments," Kate said, so Gib tucked the money in his pocket and hugged her.

"Your collar," my mother said, and fixed Gib's

collar so it didn't bunch up under his sweater. "You call us when you get there; I'll be worried about you till I know you've landed safely."

"Mom, you keep forgetting how safe it is to fly," I said. "Don't forget, Gib has to take the bus from the airport out to the college. He's much more likely to get killed on the freeway than he would be on an airplane."

My mother patted my head. "That makes me feel a lot better." She hugged Gib, then it was my father's turn.

"You have something to read on the plane?" my father asked.

"Yeah, I bought a paperback book on the making of *Star Trek*," Gib said. Then he looked at me. "Well, Poke? See you at Thanksgiving, huh?"

I nodded. "Yeah," I said. "Thanksgiving."

Gib gave me a quick hug. He started down the connecting tube to the airplane, turned, waved, then he was gone.

We stayed long enough to watch Gib's plane take off, then the four of us walked down the airport terminal and outside without saying much. I thought about Gib and me: In two days I'd be starting high school and Gib would be settling in at college. Thanksgiving would come, then Christmas break, but it'd be almost a year before we'd have a long stretch of time to go out to the airfield or to just have some fun.

The sun was white, direct, low.

It was still summer by the calendar, but not for me.

Gib was gone, and summer was over.

Part Two

10

"Pokie? You ready for school?"

Junior stood at the front door. He had on a shirt and a tie.

"Holy cow!" I said. "You're not wearing *that* to school, are you?"

"My ma's making me," he said. "You know, because they take our yearbook pictures the first day."

My mother walked into the kitchen. She was in her old robe and her hair needed a brush. "Junior? You look so nice. . . . You want to come in and have some breakfast?"

"I'm too excited to eat. My ma packed me a big lunch anyway. I got two peanut butter and marsh-

73

mallow fluff sandwiches, a bag of Chee-tos, two packs of Ding Dongs and one of Twinkies."

"Lord, I hope you don't have gym right after lunch," I said. "You'll throw up." I picked up my lunch and gave my mother a kiss. "I'll see you later."

"You two have a good first day now."

"We will. C'mon, Junior. . . ."

Junior and I were only walking to the corner together, but he made me step on every crack we came across.

"This is the last time I'm doing this," I said.

"We always step on cracks on the way to school," he said. "It's a tradition."

"It's fine for you to step on cracks because you're still in junior high. But I'm going on to the high school and high school people don't go around stepping on cracks in the sidewalk."

"Hey, Pokie . . . now that you're going to a different school I won't have anyone to eat lunch with."

"Neither will I," I said. "We'll just have to make new friends. . . ."

"Remember the fun we had in the cafeteria last year, shooting the papers off our straws? Man, that was so great!"

"Yeah, I remember. . . . Junior, you better behave yourself at school today. Sometimes you just go too far and this year I won't be around to stop you from getting into trouble—"

"I'm not gonna get in any trouble," he said. "I'm maturer than I was last year. Don't forget, I'll be in the oldest grade in my school now."

"Yeah . . . and I'll be in the youngest in mine."

"Know what I heard about the high school, Pokie?"

"No!" I said. "And don't tell me! I don't need any wild stories to scare me my first day. I'm scared enough."

"I heard that the sophomores have rigged up some sort of electric chair in one of the broom closets and whenever they feel like it, they strap a freshman in it and *zzzt!* They turn on the juice."

"Sometimes you are positively moronic, you know that?"

Junior smiled. "Thanks, Pokie."

We walked to the corner. Junior would turn right on Hawthorne and go to the junior high, and I'd go left and walk to the high school.

"Well, I guess this is it," Junior said. "I hope you like it up there at the high school."

"Me too," I said. "Make sure your tie's straight before you have your picture taken."

"I will. See you later, huh?"

"Yeah," I said. "See you later."

The high school looked completely different from the way it had the day Gib had taken me there. The halls were jam-packed and I got squeezed into the wrong room. I spent ten minutes listening to someone named Miss Ivanova speak Russian, when I should have been across the hall listening to someone named Mr. Schoen speak history. The whole morning was a disaster. During lunch I made a list of everything that had gone wrong:

1. I couldn't work my combination lock so I had to lug an armload of books to all my classes.
2. They ran out of gym suits when they came to me so I had to take P.E. in my skirt and blouse.
3. My P.E. teacher called me by my right name and everyone laughed when they heard her say "Alwilda," but no one laughed when she said, "I'm Miss Bonepeck."
4. I got lost going to English because I thought I was in the east wing, but I was really in the west wing.
5. I got in trouble in study hall for doodling airplanes even though it's the first day of school and there isn't anything to study yet.
6. I lost my English book somewhere and I can't go to the lost-and-found and see if they have it, because I don't know where the lost-and-found is.

7. I'm not in classes with any of my old friends from junior high.
8. I sat down at a small table in the cafeteria and a cheerleader dressed in a green-and-white uniform said: "I'm sorry, but my friends and I sit here every year." So I moved.
9. The cafeteria ran out of milk so I had to eat my sandwich and wash it down with warm water from the drinking fountain.
10. I don't have anyone to eat lunch with, or blow the paper off my straw with.

After school, I walked home slowly. When I came to the corner of Hawthorne and Kenilworth I saw Junior racing toward me. He had his tie off and was waving it like a maniac.

"Pokie! Hey, Pokie . . . how'd you like it? How'd you like it up there at the high school?"

"I don't know," I said.

"Man, it's so neat in the eighth grade! Guess what? I'm going to be homeroom representative in the student council—"

I stopped and looked at him. "You're *what*?"

"Yeah. Miss Swanson—you remember Miss Swanson—she says everyone made a good choice. She says I'm a born leader!"

"Lord!" I said, and started walking again, Junior right beside me.

"And during lunch I made friends with some

kid in the seventh grade and taught him how to blow the paper off his straw. He blew his straw paper right on Mr. Child's head! You remember Mr. Child, don't you?"

"For God's sake, I was just there last year! Of course I remember him! I remember all the teachers!"

"What are you getting so mad about?"

"Ever occur to you that maybe not everyone had a good first day at school? Huh? That ever *occur* to you?"

"Well, what happened up there?"

"Plenty!" I said. I ran the rest of the way, took the porch steps two at a time, went into the house, and slammed the door. My mother was sitting at the desk, talking on the phone.

"Pokie?" she said. "What's wrong?"

"I'm never going back there! I'm going to drop out of school and read every book in the library and learn things on my own!"

I ran upstairs and collapsed on the bed. I just couldn't stop crying. Pretty soon my mother was sitting beside me.

"What happened today?" she asked.

"I made a list of the morning things that went wrong," I said. "I haven't had time to write down all the afternoon things yet." I sat up and pulled the list out of my notebook and handed it to her. She read it carefully and smiled when she finished.

"The first day at anything new is always the hardest," she said.

"It's not fair," I said. "I hate high school and Junior's having a great time in the eighth grade and I miss Gib. It's not fair."

"Gib's on the phone right now. He called just to see how your first day went."

"Really?"

"You better go talk to him; he got worried when I told him how upset you were—"

I picked up the phone. "Gib?"

"Hell, Poke, what happened today? Mom says you're really unhappy about something—"

"Everything went wrong, Gib. I got lost and didn't make a single friend or have anyone to eat lunch with—"

"Poke, it was just like that for me here at college, too—"

"It was?"

"Sure. It's just going to take a while for us, Poke. You'll see. By the end of the week things'll start working out—"

"Thanks, Gib."

Gib was right. Things *did* start working out: On Tuesday I made a new friend, a girl named Lily. She was in line with me at the cafeteria. She walked over to the empty table reserved for the cheerleader and sat down. "Want to eat together?"

"We can't sit here," I said. "This table belongs to a cheerleader and her friends."

"We can sit anywhere we want," she said. "Let them find another table."

So the two of us sat down to eat together.

Other things started working out, too: By Wednesday I learned to work my combination, by Thursday I didn't get lost once, and by Friday I decided maybe I wouldn't drop out after all.

Maybe I'd just stick around and get an education.

11

Hi, Poke!

I'm sitting in the student union having a Coke and taking a break between classes. I've got a few minutes before political science, so I have time to get a letter off to you.

I'm finally settled in here at school. I've got a weird roommate from California named Neil and I guess he thought Missouri was on the ocean because he brought his surfboard! Can you believe that? He's got it propped up in the corner of our room.

I've been meeting a lot of other people, though, who are pretty cool. I met a guy from

New York whose father is a pilot. We had a good time talking about airplanes.

I really miss you! I hope everything's going okay for you at school. Tell Kate I really liked the care package she sent. Neil ate some of the cookies and said they were "Mondo Fantastico!" which I guess is California talk for "great."

Give my love to everyone.

Love,
Gib

I took a break from raking the front yard to show Junior the letter from Gib. I'd been carrying it around in my back pocket ever since I'd gotten it. We sat on the porch steps while Junior read the letter. It was a beautiful sunny-cold day, the beginning of fall. I had a huge pile of orange and gold leaves raked in the middle of the yard.

Junior handed the letter back to me and frowned. "Gib doesn't say anything about *me*," he said.

"Well, sure he does," I said. "He says, 'Give my love to everyone.' That includes you, too."

"You think Gib's forgotten my name, Pokie?"

"Of course he hasn't forgotten your name!" I said. "Lord, he's lived next door to you since the day you were born! It's just that he's busy now. He's in college and he's very busy."

"Gib should have a secretary like the movie stars do. That way, the secretary could handle his mail, and Gib could spend all his time studying."

I looked at him. "Where do you get these ideas of yours?"

Junior smiled. "They just pop right into my brain," he said. "Hey, Pokie . . . you want to go downtown and look at the store windows? They're starting to paint them for Halloween."

"No, I'm gonna spend this afternoon setting my hair."

"Setting your hair! What do you want to do *that* for?"

"Because I want my hair curled, if it's all right with you."

Junior thought a second. "I guess it's all right with me."

"Thanks!" I said.

"Can I jump in your pile of leaves, Pokie?"

"Aren't you a little big for that?"

"No," he said. "Can I? I'll rake 'em up again."

"Go ahead. . . ."

Junior climbed up on the porch railing and jumped right into the center of the leaf pile and squashed it flat. "Come on, Pokie, this is fun! I'll get 'em in a pile again and you try it—"

"Well, maybe just once," I said. Junior took the rake and pushed the leaves into a big pile. I got up on the porch railing and jumped into the leaves just like he had.

"We used to do this all the time, remember?" Junior said.

"Help me up," I said. I held out my hand and Junior took it. I pulled him down into the leaf pile.

"Neat, Pokie! Do it again!"

I threw some leaves at him. "I'm tired!" I said. "I've been raking all morning." We stayed there a minute, half buried in the crispy leaves. "What's going on with your student council job?" I asked. "You haven't mentioned it lately."

"Oh, that," Junior said. "I quit it."

"Quit it! How come?"

"The kids in my homeroom thought my ideas were a big joke so I quit."

"What ideas?"

"Well, I had this idea of putting Kool-Aid in the drinking fountains instead of water. Don't you think that's a good idea?"

I couldn't help smiling. "They made fun of that?"

"Yeah. They laughed at me and it made my feelings hurt so I quit."

"I'm sorry you got your feelings hurt."

I suddenly noticed Kate standing over us. "I've been baking pound cake all morning and I need a couple of tasters. You two interested?"

"Yeah!" Junior said. He jumped up and started brushing the leaves off his pants.

84

Kate grabbed my hands and pulled me to my feet. She helped me pick the leaves out of my hair.

"Kate, do you think my hair'll look good curled? I eat lunch with a girl named Lily and she wears her hair curled almost every day."

"I think it'd look nice that way," Kate said. "You should bring your friend Lily around sometime."

"What does she need Lily for, Pokie's Gramma?" Junior asked. "She's got me."

"Yes," I said, "but your hair's not curly."

"Very funny," Junior said.

October 20th

Dear Gib,

I can't wait till you come home next month! I'm doing okay at school. I made a friend named Lily in the cafeteria and I'm going to ask her to come over sometime next week.

I have to write a short story for English so I'm writing about a girl my age who gets her pilot's license and saves her town by crop-dusting the corn so it doesn't get attacked by giant killer bees. I got the giant killer bee idea from watching *Science Fiction Theater* last week, but the idea about crop-dusting is my own.

Junior's starting to get on my nerves. He's afraid you've forgotten about him because you didn't mention him in your letter. I told him how silly that was, but you know how Junior is.

I wish you were here. I don't have anyone to talk to about airplanes. When I try to talk to Junior about them, his eyes glaze over.

I miss you.

Love,
Pokie

Lily came home with me the next Monday after school. My mother and Kate were at the dining-room table. They had papers and envelopes spread out all over the place; it looked like they were doing more work for the League of Women Voters. I introduced Lily to them, and I was kind of embarrassed because my mother had kicked off her shoes and was sitting there in her bare feet.

"You girls help yourself to cookies or whatever," my mother said, so Lily and I went into the kitchen and found a package of Oreos and a couple of cans of Fresca.

"I'll set your hair if you want," Lily said. "You got any Dippity-Do?"

"I think my mother might. Come on."

We went upstairs and while Lily was halfway through winding my hair up on rollers, Junior stuck his ugly face in my window. It nearly scared the socks off me. I raced over and shoved the window up.

"Hey there, Pokie. What are you doing?"

"Junior Hollinger, how'd you get *up* here?"

"I climbed up the trellis and I'm standing on the gutter."

"Shoot, you better get in here before you break your neck!" I slid the screen up and Lily and I pulled Junior inside. "You must be crazy!" I said. "What's wrong with the doorbell, huh?"

"I just started climbing, Pokie. I didn't know where I was going to end up. Honest."

"Aren't you going to introduce us, Pokie?" Lily asked.

"You don't want to be introduced to him," I said.

"Sure, I do," Lily said. "Don't you ever read the etiquette lady in the paper? She says the hostess should always introduce guests to each other—"

"Junior's no guest," I said, but I introduced them fast, then dragged Junior downstairs and chucked him out the door.

"Why can't I stay?"

"You don't understand about setting hair and Dippity-Do."

"You better be careful setting your hair on those rollers, Pokie. I remember hearing about a girl who had her rollers wound so tight she ended up with her eyes crossed. Permanently."

"Just go find something else to do, okay?"

"Come on, Pokie . . . why can't we hang around together like we always do?"

"Because things are different now," I said. "We don't have to do every single thing together."

I shut the door in his face. I felt a little bad about that. Not a lot, but a little.

When I got back upstairs, Lily said, "He's kind of cute."

"Junior?"

She nodded and went to work on my hair.

Lily thought Junior was "cute." I couldn't believe it.

But then I remembered something Kate had said to me once: "To each his own, the old lady said as she kissed the cow."

I guess Junior just happened to be Lily's cow.

12

Junior invited himself over for lunch one Saturday. He made a big peanut butter and banana sandwich, stuffed half of it into his mouth, then sat there and talked with his mouth full. It was disgusting.

"Gib sent me a postcard, Pokie," Junior said. "Know what he wrote? He wrote, 'Keep an eye on Pokie and make sure she stays out of trouble.' Isn't that a riot! 'Make sure she stays out of trouble'!"

"If you ever read the etiquette lady in the paper you'd know it's very bad manners to laugh with your mouth full," I said.

"You never used to care about the etiquette lady

in the paper until you started hanging around with that girl Lily," Junior said. "You aren't the same since you started curling your hair."

"You're just jealous because I have a new friend."

Junior didn't say anything for a minute. He worked on his sandwich. "Suppose you don't want to go out trick-or-treating with me, either—"

"I'm too old for that," I said.

"You're too old for everything since you started high school."

"I can't help it if I'm growing up," I said.

"I'm going as a giant mouse," he said. "I even got me a giant piece of cheese I'm going to carry."

I felt good and guilty. "Well, I guess I could come along. You know, sort of to keep you company."

"You really want to?"

"Sure. But I'm not dressing up in any costume."

Halloween night I was in the kitchen making popcorn balls for the trick-or-treaters. My father stuck his head in the door and grinned.

"Pokie? There's a mouse out here waiting for you."

"Do I have to go with him, Dad? I said I would, but I'll feel stupid traipsing around the neighborhood with a giant mouse."

"What'd you go as last year?" my father asked.

"A bird or something—"

"Tweetie Bird," I said. "From the cartoons."

"That's right," my father said.

"I wouldn't be caught dead in that costume now."

"A year makes a big difference."

"I guess Junior won't be trick-or-treating after this year," I said. I handed my father the bowl of popcorn balls. "I guess it won't hurt me to go with him. I just hope he doesn't make me carry the cheese."

Junior carried his own cheese. I walked along behind him and watched his tail drag on the sidewalk.

"How come you wanted to go as a mouse?" I asked. "Most of the other boys your age are dressed as normal Halloween stuff. You know. Monsters or axe murderers or something."

"I've wanted to be a mouse ever since I found this costume up in the attic. My pop was a mouse when he was my age."

"Oh."

"Mice run in our family, Pokie."

"Very cute. Ha ha."

"Hey, Pokie, remember last year when we went trick-or-treating and you beat up the kid who stole our candy?"

"I didn't beat him up," I said. "Not exactly. I just socked him in the stomach is all."

"Man, that was so funny! Tweetie Bird knocking the heck out of Frankenstein!"

"Pokie!" I heard Lily yell. I turned and saw her across the street. She waved and ran over to us. "I'm glad I caught up with you. Your mom said you were out trick-or-treating but I didn't believe it—"

"I'm not trick-or-treating," I said. "I'm just keeping Junior company while *he* does it."

"Is that you under there, Junior?" Lily asked, and Junior pushed back his mouse head.

"Yeah," he said. "It's me."

"Pokie, you want to come over for a while?" Lily said. "Some friends and I are gonna make a haunted house and let the trick-or-treaters go through it. You want to help us?"

I looked at Junior. "I don't know . . ."

"Well, you can come along, too, Junior," Lily said.

Junior pulled his mouse head back on. "No, thanks. You go on if you want to, Pokie."

He walked away from us. "I'll be right back, Lily," I said. I hurried and caught up with Junior. "Junior, wait a second . . . don't you want to go over to Lily's house?"

He turned and looked at me. I could just see his eyes through the eyeholes cut out in the costume. "We were going around alone tonight, Pokie. Just the two of us. Like we always do."

"What difference does it make if we're out

alone or if we're out with other people?"

"It makes a big difference," he said. "I don't want to hang around those high school kids. I want to hang around you."

"Come on, Junior. It'll be fun—"

He shrugged. "I told you. Go ahead if you want to."

"Junior, you drive me crazy sometimes. Now, just tell me. Do you want me to go or *not*?"

Junior shook his mouse head at me. "No, Pokie. I don't want you to go."

I took a deep breath. "I'm going," I said.

"Go on then," he said. "I was going to share half of my treats with you, but now I'm not so sure." He threw his tail over his shoulder and marched off. I felt totally stupid, getting told off by a giant mouse like that. I walked back to Lily.

"Isn't he coming?" she asked.

"No. Don't ask me why. I just can't figure him out these days."

We started walking toward Lily's house. When I looked over my shoulder, Junior was heading in the opposite direction. I hadn't realized how tall he was getting, and it was kind of sad the way he towered over the other trick-or-treaters. Junior didn't want anything to change. He'd probably want to go on trick-or-treating till he was forty, and he'd want our friendship to stay the same forever.

But our friendship was already changing.

We were both growing up. It couldn't be helped and it couldn't be stopped.

Why couldn't he get that through his head?

13

Gib came home the day before Thanksgiving. My parents and I drove out to O'Hare to meet his plane. The airport was packed with holiday travelers, but I just shoved my way around the crowds and hurried toward Gib's gate, something my parents seemed unwilling to do.

"Will you guys please hurry *up*?" I said. "What's Gib going to think when he gets off the plane and there's no one there to greet him?"

"I don't think your mom and I feel like running," my father said. "You go on ahead. We'll catch up with you."

I hurried. I ran. When I got to the gate, Gib's

DC-10 had just docked with the airport tunnel. The doors swung open and the passengers started pushing past me. I elbowed my way through the crowd and spotted Gib halfway down the tunnel. "Gib!" I yelled. "Over here!"

He looked my way and smiled. He was wearing a khaki hat and his hair was a little longer than when he'd left. I ran to him and he dropped the backpack he was carrying and gave me a hug that lifted me off my feet.

"Poke! Look at you! You've grown a foot!"

"No, I haven't," I said. "You've just got me up in the air!"

"Oh, yeah. . . ." He set me down, took off his hat, and put it on my head. "Where are Mom and Dad? You didn't drive out here by yourself, did you?"

"Hell, no!" I said. "But I could have gotten us out here a lot faster than Dad did. He and Mom even walk slow; they're back there some-where—"

"Brought you something," Gib said. He un-zipped his backpack and pulled out a yellow sweatshirt. It had "University of Missouri" printed on the front, and "Pokie" printed on the back.

"This is great! Thanks, Gib."

He picked up his backpack and we started walking.

"You're doing something different to your hair," Gib said.

"Yeah, I set it on rollers every night. Do you like it?"

"Makes you look a lot older."

"Really?"

"You look like a college girl."

"Gib, there's Mom and Dad."

He went to our parents and got a double hug from them.

"Look at your hair!" my mother said. "Don't they have barbers in Missouri?"

Gib laughed. "I've been so busy I haven't had time to get it cut. . . . Where's Kate?"

"She's doing some baking for tomorrow," my mother said. "She wants you to go over as soon as we get home—"

I held up my sweatshirt. "Look what Gib brought me—"

"A friend of mine works in a T-shirt shop near the campus," he said. "She printed it up for me—"

"She?" my father said. "Is this a *good* friend, Gib?"

Gib ducked his head shyly. "Just a friend, Dad."

My father grinned and threw his arm around Gib's shoulders. We headed back down the terminal and I caught sight of our reflections in some glass doors.

I wasn't exactly like Junior. I knew things had

to change, and Gib's life at college was one of them, but right now I wanted us to stay just like we were in the window reflections.

The four of us, together.

Just like it used to be.

14

Junior managed to finish eating Thanksgiving dinner with his family and make it over to our house before we'd even started ours. My mother set a place for him at the table.

"Do we have to let him stay?" I whispered to her. "It'd be doing him a favor to kick him out. He'll get sick eating two turkey dinners."

"Junior's a bottomless pit and you know it," my mother said. "I think he just wants to visit with Gib. It won't hurt to let him stay—"

"It might," I said.

Junior sat between Gib and me. He drove me crazy—he just wouldn't stop asking Gib questions.

"Hey, Gib," he said. "They let you chew gum down there at college?"

Everyone at the table burst out laughing. Junior did, too, but he had a confused kind of look that showed he didn't know what he was laughing at.

"No, really, Gib," he said. "I want to know all about college. I might want to go down there if they let you chew gum—"

"I guess you can chew gum if you want," Gib said. "In one of my classes there's a girl who sits in the back and knits during lectures—"

"I don't know how to knit," Junior said. "But I know how to make a fort out of toothpicks."

"Lord!" I said. "You don't go to college to make toothpick forts!"

"Well, I can make lots of other things out of toothpicks besides forts. I made a birdhouse one time, but none of the birds wanted to go inside it."

Junior and his toothpick stories were from outer space. Here was Gib, fresh home from college, with probably a million interesting experiences to tell us about, and somehow we were stuck listening to a twelve-year-old from the planet Demento. I think we were all relieved when the phone rang.

"I'll get it!" I said. I ran into the kitchen and picked up the phone.

"Hello?" I said.

"Could I talk to Gib, please?" a girl's voice said.

"Oh . . . just a minute." I couldn't figure out what girl would be calling Gib on Thanksgiving. I went to the door. "Gib? It's for you. Some girl."

"You got a girlfriend, Gib?" Junior said, and Gib smiled and threw his napkin at Junior. "Eat your turkey."

"Okay," Junior said.

Gib came into the kitchen and picked up the phone. He looked at me. "This is kind of private, Poke."

"Oh," I said. I went back out to the dining room and sat down.

"Who was it?" Junior asked.

"She didn't say."

"Bet Gib went and got himself a girlfriend down there at school."

"Suppose that's another reason you want to go to college now, huh?" I said.

Junior shoveled a big spoonful of mashed potatoes into his mouth. "Yeah!" he said.

Gib had never had a girlfriend, not a real one, not one he had to have a private phone conversation with. That night while he was watching a Laurel and Hardy movie in the family room I went and sat down next to him.

"*The Flying Deuces*," Gib said. "The one where they join the Foreign Legion."

"Oh, yeah," I said. We watched the blue-black shadows of Laurel and Hardy on the screen.

"Gib? Who was that girl on the phone? Is she your girlfriend?"

Gib put his hands behind his head and stretched his legs out on the coffee table. "She's not exactly a girlfriend," he said. "We're just dating. I met her in poli. sci."

"What's poli. sci.?"

"Political science."

"Well, what's her name?"

"Nell."

"Oh."

"Potts."

"Oh."

"She's from Independence, Missouri."

"Oh."

We went back to watching the movie. I got caught up in Stan and Ollie doing a dance to the song "Shine On, Harvest Moon." Gib and I started laughing hard. We were carrying on like we always had. Nothing had changed.

For the time being, I forgot all about this friend of Gib's.

I forgot all about Nell, the girl from Independence.

15

December 13th

Dear Gib,

Guess what. I'm going to the Snowflake Dance at school. My friend Lily and I waited all week to get asked to it by some boys, but since no boys asked us we decided to go together and that way we won't have to walk into the gym alone.

Mom and Kate took me to Oakbrook and bought me a dress at Marshall Field. I swear, that's the last time I go shopping with those two. Kate liked one dress, Mom liked another. This is the way their conversation went:

"What do you think of *this* dress?" Mom asked Kate.

"Pink washes Pokie out," Kate said. "It's not a good color for her. How about this?" Kate held up a dress and Mom made a face.

"You're not *serious*, Mother," she said. "That's black. She's going to a school dance, not a cocktail party—"

"It's not black," Kate said. "It's navy."

"It's black."

"It just *looks* black under these lights. It's really navy."

I stood there and listened to them go back and forth like that, like I wasn't even there. Finally I went and picked out a dress *I* liked. "I like *this* dress," I said. "When you two go to a dance *you* can pick out the dresses."

Then, the worst: They started laughing. The kind of laughter where there were tears in their eyes and they were doubled over. The saleslady gave them a funny look and I didn't blame her. I wanted to be a million miles away from them.

From now on, I shop alone.

I'll let you know how I like the dance. Junior's coming over tomorrow afternoon and show me some steps. He went to Bobby Rivers' Dance School last year and was the best in his class, or so he says! You know Junior!

I can't wait till Christmas. No school, but best of all, you'll be home again.

Don't work too hard.

Love,
Pokie

Junior turned out to be a very bad dance teacher. I ended up with stepped-on toes and somehow he managed to give me a cramp in my hand.

"Enough!" I said. "Let's stop for a minute." I snapped off the radio we'd been listening to and sat on the couch. "Thought you were supposed to be the best dancer in your class."

"I was, Pokie," Junior said. "Honest. Something must have happened since last year."

"Well, you're a lot taller, for one thing. Maybe it's thrown your coordination off." When Junior and I stood together these days, we were eye to nose. For the first time since I'd known him, he was taller than I.

"I've grown three inches since summer," he said. "When I get up there to the high school I'm gonna try out for the basketball team."

"I didn't know you liked basketball," I said.

"I don't. But what good is being tall if I can't do anything with it?"

"Junior Hollinger, basketball champion."

"Yep, that's right," Junior said. "Hey, Pokie—

you think maybe I could come along with you when you go to the dance? That way, you'll have someone to dance with—"

"What makes you think no one's going to ask me to dance?"

"Well, Pokie," he said in a serious tone, "I mean, you just might not get asked. There's always lots of girls at dances that sit there and never get asked and you might be one of them."

"I'm not going to be one of them."

"Wallflowers. That's that they call 'em."

"Junior, sometimes you just go on and on—"

"Why do you think they call girls who don't get asked to dance wallflowers? Doesn't make sense. I think they should call them chairsitters, because that's what they do. They sit on chairs." He turned to me and smiled. "I always like it when I figure something out."

"Lord!" I said.

"So can I come, Pokie?"

"No," I said. "This is a high school dance for high school people and they wouldn't let you in—"

"I bet they'd let me in if you told 'em I was your cousin from France—"

"France!"

"Well, sure. If I was from France they might let me in. People are always nice to visitors from other countries."

"If you want people to be nice to you, maybe

you better tell them you're from outer space," I said. " 'Cause you are."

Junior laughed. "Outer space! I like that, Pokie."

"Yeah," I said. "I thought you would."

The lights in the gym were dimmed; red and green crepe-paper streamers hung from the ceiling. The basketball hoops were decorated with tiny white fairy lights. Rock music blared from the P.A. system and made the floor vibrate. There were a bunch of wallflowers, or chairsitters, as Junior would call them, on one side of the gym.

"Wonder how come there aren't any boys waiting to be asked to dance," Lily said.

"Because there are more girls than boys here, looks like."

"Want to dance?" someone said, and Lily and I turned around. A boy with a nice face and a space between his teeth was looking at Lily. "Want to?"

"Sure," she said, and they walked over to the center of the gym and started dancing. I went over to the refreshment table and got some punch from the P.T.A. ladies. Then I didn't know what to do, so I went over and sat with the other girls who weren't chosen. I was a chairsitter, just like Junior had predicted. I sat there for a half hour. I looked down at my feet. I was wearing my new black patent leather flats and they pinched my toes so I slipped them off.

"Um, Pokie, right?"

I looked up at a familiar face, a boy from my history class.

"Yeah," I said. "Right."

"Want to dance?"

"Yes. Sure." I stood up and started to walk out onto the dance floor, then I remembered my shoes. "My shoes," I said. "My feet hurt so I took them off."

"Hey, that's a great idea!" he said. He pulled his shoes off and tossed them next to mine. "Now we can step on each other's feet and it won't hurt."

Neither of us was very good at dancing, but that was okay. I was more worried about what to say to him.

"I liked your Civil War report," I said.

"I liked yours, too."

We danced a little more.

"That was some war, wasn't it?" I asked.

"Yeah," he said. "It really was."

December 17th

Dear Gib,

The dance was great. The first boy I danced with is in my history class. I didn't know what to talk to him about, so I talked about the Civil War we'd been studying. After I danced with the Civil War boy, I danced with three others. I ended up spending the evening talking about things like the Constitution, *Ol-*

iver Twist, frog anatomy, and algebraic equations.

This social stuff is a killer, Gib. It's not the dancing I mind so much. It's remembering everything I've learned in school so I have something to talk to my dancing partners about. God knows what grown-ups talk about at cocktail parties. They must study weeks in advance.

Won't be long before you're on Christmas break. See you then!

Love,
Pokie

16

Gib gave me a silver necklace for Christmas. It had a little airplane dangling from it, and the airplane had tiny propellers on it that moved.

"I've never seen anything so pretty," I said. I fastened it around my neck. "Where'd you find it, Gib?"

"At a little store near the school."

We were sitting around the tree, all of us still in our pajamas and robes. Kate had thrown her coat over her nightgown and come over that way. She and my parents sat wearing some of their Christmas presents: My father wore a wool muffler, my mother had a knit cap on, and Kate was trying on some black gloves. Gib and I made out a lot better. We got some of the typical boring Christmas underwear and socks, but my parents had also given me a deluxe model airplane kit with enough parts to make a radio-controlled airplane. They'd given Gib one of those fancy radios that carried the weather and police bands.

Gib was unwrapping his present from me. I'd gotten him a World War II aviator jacket, just like the one Hank Jellies had. I'd found it at Kohler's Trading Post in an old trunk. It was too expensive, but my dad helped me out with it.

"Poke, this is fantastic!" Gib said. He stood up and put it on.

"You can wear it when you make your first solo flight," I said.

"I will. Thanks."

There was a knock on the door. I jumped up and opened it and said "Merry Christmas!" before I even knew who it was.

"Merry Christmas, Pokie." Junior Hollinger walked right on inside. He held a Saran Wrapped fruitcake in his hand. "My ma sent me over with this."

"Thank you, Junior," my mother said. "I have some Christmas cookies for you if you'll wait a second." She took the fruitcake from him and went into the kitchen.

Junior's eyes swept over us. "Holy mackerel! It's almost noon and no one's dressed!"

"You make us sound like a nudist camp," I said.

"A nudist camp!" Junior said. "Pretty funny, Pokie. What'd you get for Christmas?"

"Gib gave me this necklace and I got a kit for making a radio-controlled airplane."

"You look mighty snazzy, Junior Hollinger," Kate said. "Is that jacket a Christmas present?"

"Yeah, Pokie's Gramma. And I got a toboggan sled, too." He looked at Gib and me. "I'm going over to the hill on Linden and try it out. You guys want to come with me?"

"Yeah!" I said. "Come on, Gib—"

"I better hang around the house today," he said. "I might get a phone call."

"Who from?" Junior said, and then he grinned. "I know . . . that girlfriend of yours down there in Missouri—"

Gib smiled, but I noticed a light rose-colored blush spreading over his face. It wasn't like Gib to embarrass easily, so Junior's remark must have had some meaning to it, to make him change color like that.

"I'll go get dressed and meet you on the hill in a few minutes," I said. "I'll bring my sled and we can have a race."

"Okay," Junior said. "See you in a few minutes."

My sled was an old one with rusty runners. It was no match for Junior's brand-new toboggan.

"You'll never get anywhere on that," he said. "Come on. You can ride with me."

112

I sat behind Junior and put my arms around his waist. The sky was a bright-blue winter sky, and we had the whole hill to ourselves. We leaned forward and went sailing. We were flying, really, without even leaving the ground. When we got to the bottom of the hill we climbed off the sled and trudged back up to the top again, pulling the sled behind us. We went down four more times.

"Let's sit a minute," I said. "I'm getting tired."

We sat sideways on the sled, with our legs sticking out in the snow.

"Hey, Pokie," Junior said. "You know, Gib's not the only one who has himself a girlfriend."

"*You* have a girlfriend?"

"Uh huh. We eat lunch together."

"What's her name?"

"I don't know."

"You don't know your own girlfriend's name?"

"Not yet."

"Oh, brother," I said. "Something tells me there's no girlfriend, just some girl who probably sits at the same table you do. I'll bet she doesn't even talk to you."

"She does, too. She asked me to stop staring at her."

I pointed a finger at him. "You're gonna get in trouble someday with those stories you tell," I said. "Serious trouble."

"I don't tell stories," he said. "Not exactly. I just fancy up the truth a little."

"A little!" I said.

"Pokie, you could be my girlfriend, maybe."

"Me! I most certainly could not!"

"Well, why not? I'm not that much younger—"

"When *I* date someone," I said, "it'll be someone from my own species."

"No, really, Pokie, why couldn't you? If we're boyfriend and girlfriend and if we get married sometime, we can look back on this day and remember it was the day we decided to fall in love."

"See, this is what I mean," I said. "This just shows how much you don't know about things. You can't decide to fall in love. It just happens."

"All right," he said. "Then how about kissing me once. You know, try out my lips and see how you like them."

"Junior Hollinger, I swear—"

"Come on, Pokie. Just one kiss—"

"If I kiss you once will you stop all this boyfriend-girlfriend talk?"

"Yeah, I promise."

I pressed my lips against Junior's, and after our first kiss he sat back and shook his head. "Maybe it's better if we're just friends," he said.

Gib was supposed to be home for two weeks during Christmas break, but it didn't exactly work out that way. The day after New Year's I came home from an afternoon at Kate's to find Gib in the middle of an argument with my mother. My father was there, too, but it looked like he couldn't get a word in edgewise.

"I just don't like the idea, Gib," my mother said.

"Come on, Mom," Gib said. "I'll be going back to school in a few days anyway—"

"What's going on?" I asked.

Gib looked at me. "My friend Nell called and invited me to spend the rest of vacation with her and her family in Independence—"

"You're not *going*, are you, Gib?" I asked. "Seems like you only just got home—"

"I know, Poke, but this is something I really want to do."

My father and mother were looking at each other. I knew that look: They were about to cave in.

"You're going to let him go, *aren't* you?" I said. "I don't think that's fair!" I ran upstairs. I was good and mad. I sat on my bed and tapped my foot and tried to calm down. It seemed like I'd been waiting since summer to spend some time with Gib and now he was leaving again.

I heard Gib's footsteps on the stairs, then I noticed him standing in the doorway. "You're not really mad about me leaving, are you, Poke?"

"Yes," I said. "I think Mom and Dad are crazy to let you go use up your vacation on strangers."

"Well, Dad says it's all part of college life. He told Mom and me that story again . . . you know, the one about how he visited his college roommate Spider down in Mississippi one Christmas and they served grits with everything he ate—"

"Oh, yeah, the grits story," I said. "Gib? How much do you like this girl, anyway? Junior keeps calling her your girlfriend. Is she?"

"I guess she's my girlfriend," Gib said. "I guess it's working out that way. You'd like Nell, Poke. She's a lot of fun."

"What kind of fun? Is she good at telling jokes?"

"Well, no. But she likes to laugh at them."

"Oh."

"I better go start packing. My plane leaves at four."

"Aren't Mom and Dad taking you out to the airport?"

"Mom needs the car this afternoon so I'm taking the airport limousine. They're coming in an hour."

When Gib left in the airport limousine he wore the aviator jacket I'd given him for Christmas. My parents and I stood at the door and waved goodbye, and he waved back, but he wasn't really seeing us. His mind was on other things.

It was funny: Gib was part of our family still, and yet he wasn't. I couldn't put my finger on it exactly, I only knew that there was some distance now between him and us.

Distance that never used to be there.

17

February 10th

Dear Gib,

I thought I better get this letter off to you fast, and maybe it'll get there before the care package does. I sent you a batch of chocolate-chip cookies, only I realized after I mailed them that I forgot to put the chocolate chips in. I'm worried that they may taste like there's something missing. Junior was standing next to me while I was trying to make the cookies, and his talk-talk-talk got me so confused I didn't know what I was doing. Next time I'll send him home so I can bake in peace.

Junior's all excited because he's in the spring talent show at school. He's going to sing a solo version of "I Won't Grow Up," from *Peter Pan*. I think he chose the perfect song for him!

Last week Dad and I went outside to fly my radio-controlled airplane. It buzzed around fine until Dad took the controls; then it crashed into a tree and almost hit a squirrel on the head. I felt kind of bad for him when he said it was a good thing he wasn't a real pilot.

I hope you're not studying too hard.

Love,
Pokie

February 18th

Hi, Poke,

Thanks for the cookies. I thought they tasted great, and I didn't miss the chocolate chips at all.

I should have warned you a long time ago not to let Dad fly any of your planes. When I was little he and I built a radio-controlled helicopter together, and he flew it too near my head and it chopped some of my hair off. Ever since then I've been afraid to let him get his hands on any of my airplanes unless I've had a hat on.

Tell Junior congratulations on getting that

part in the talent show. That's one perform-
ance I'd give anything to see.

Wish this could be longer, but I've got two
exams coming up so I better start cracking
the books.

Miss you.

Love,
Gib

February 25th
Dear Poke,

I hope you won't be too mad if I don't come
home for spring break. One of my professors
volunteers for a group that helps homeless
people build houses, and a bunch of kids
from college are going to spend spring break
helping him. It seems like a worthwhile thing
for me to do, Poke. I want college to be more
than just studying and partying. I want to do
something for people who aren't as lucky as
you and me. I'm going to talk to Mom and
Dad about this, but I wanted to let you know
ahead of time.

Love,
Gib

"*I* can tell you why Gib's not coming home,"
Junior said. "It's that girl of his. Bet *she's* not
going home for spring break, either."

"Well, it's clear you don't understand about helping humanity and all that," I said. "Maybe you will once you're older, but I doubt it."

"Gib's going to be hammering nails with one hand and hugging that girlfriend of his with the other."

"Shut up," I said. "You don't know what you're talking about."

"Well, I really do, Pokie," Junior said. "I watch a lot of television."

March 7th

Dear Gib,

I think it's wonderful about you helping those people, but I'll miss you on spring vacation. Mom says we'll plan a few things to do, like go into the Museum of Science and Industry. I always enjoy walking through the giant heart. Junior's already invited himself along. He can't wait to see the pickled babies, his favorite part of the museum. I know what you're doing on spring break is more important than going to a museum, but I guess I'm selfish or something because I wish you were coming home instead of helping society.

Love,
Pokie

Dear Pokie,

Hello! I wanted to write to you and introduce myself. My name is Nell Potts (I'm a friend of Gib's). Gib has told me so much about you, I feel like I know you. I know you love airplanes and you hate asparagus, so we have something in common (I hate asparagus too).

I'm not as lucky as Gib; I'm an only child. I always wanted a brother or sister. My mama and papa and I are from Independence, Missouri. (That's the town where President Harry Truman grew up.)

I'm studying lots of different things, but I think one day I might want to be a lawyer, although I'm not sure yet. Gib says you want to be a pilot, and I think it's great that you know what you want to be at such a young age.

Right now I work part-time in a T-shirt shop to help pay for college. I printed up the "Pokie" on that sweatshirt Gib got for you. I hope you had as much fun wearing it as I had designing it.

I guess I've talked enough! I just wanted to write and say hello to Gib's sister.

Sincerely,
Nell Potts

I showed Nell's letter to Junior.

"Why do you suppose she wrote me?" I asked.

Junior looked up from the letter. "I didn't know you hated asparagus," he said.

I frowned. "Forget about that," I said. "What about the letter? Why do you suppose she wrote me this letter?"

"Pokie, you should taste my ma's asparagus. She melts this cheese stuff on it and you can hardly even tell it's asparagus."

"For God's sake, I can't *believe* you read that whole letter and the only thing you got out of it is asparagus!"

Junior squinted hard at the letter. "She has real nice handwriting, Pokie. Wonder how she gets her *l*'s so loopy like that—"

"*You're* the one who's loopy," I said.

I folded the letter and stuffed it back into its envelope.

"Well, it's just a letter, after all," Junior said. "I mean, there's nothing to get upset about."

"I'm not upset. Just seems odd to get a letter from a person I don't even know—"

"Could be she wants to be your pen pal," Junior said. "You should write her back."

"What'll I tell her?"

"Want me to help you write it?"

"I'm not sure," I said. "I might let you help me."

"Let's both write her a letter," Junior said. "And we'll mail the best one."

That seemed like a pretty good idea to me. "Okay," I said.

Junior knocked off his letter in about ten minutes, but I struggled over mine for a half hour. When I was finished, we traded each other's letters and read them. This was Junior's letter:

March 20th

Dear Nell,
   Thank you for writing me and telling me about yourself. Now I will tell you a little about myself. When I'm not in school, I like to spend time with my best friend, Junior Hollinger.
   Junior is a tall, good-looking boy with spiky cut hair and a wonderful singing voice. He was chosen to appear in the junior high's spring talent show, and there are rumors that a talent scout from one of the big movie studios may be in the audience. I know it's only a question of time before Junior becomes famous and gets a star on Hollywood Boulevard. When he does, I plan on visiting Hollywood twice a year to scrape the gum off his star and keep it polished.
   Well, I hope this has told you a little about me.

Yours very truly,
Pokie

My brains hurt after reading that letter. I handed it back to Junior and looked at him. "You can't be serious," I said.

"What's wrong with it?"

"This is a letter about *you*, not *me*," I said.

He looked over the letter. "Oh."

"And none of the stuff in that letter is true," I said. "You just make up any old thing that comes into your head."

"I suppose your letter's better," he said.

"Yes, it's better," I said.

This was *my* letter:

March 20th

Dear Nell,

Thank you for writing me. It's very interesting that you live in the same town one of our presidents once lived in. I hope you become a lawyer someday like you want to. I'm glad Gib has a friend down there at college, and I hope I get to meet you sometime.

Sincerely,
Pokie

"You call *that* a letter?" Junior asked.

"Yes," I said. I addressed an envelope, then Junior and I walked down to the corner and dropped it in the mailbox. I didn't particularly want to answer Nell's letter, but she was a friend of Gib's, so I sort of had to.

You do things for your brother.

18

I got myself pretty dressed up for Junior's talent show. I wore a light-blue flowered dress and white flats. I tried to French braid my hair, but I couldn't do it so I settled for a plain old American ponytail.

"Pokie?" my mother said. She peeked into my room. "Is Junior in here?"

"Here? No . . ."

"His mother's on the phone. She can't find him anywhere and he's due up at the school for the talent show—"

"Well, I knew it," I said. "He's been talking about that talent show for two months, and now the day comes and he's chickening out—"

"You have any idea where he might be?"

"I'm not sure," I said. "I'll go look for him, though."

I thought he might be under his porch, the place I'd hidden the day I dented the fender, but he wasn't there.

"Junior Hollinger!" I yelled. "Come on out!"

I looked around his yard, in the garage, behind the hedges. Then I thought of the treehouse. I walked to it slowly, and I was pretty sure I saw the toe of Junior's shoe sticking out over the edge of the platform.

"Junior Hollinger, you come down from there," I said. "You want to fall off and bang yourself up like *I* did last summer?"

The toe disappeared.

"Thought you wanted all those talent agents to hear you sing," I said.

"There aren't any talent agents," Junior's voice said. "I just made that up."

"Shoot, don't you think I know that? Stick your head over here so I can see you."

Slowly Junior's face appeared over the edge of the platform.

"I got all dressed up, just for you," I said. "I even did my hair up in a ponytail, see?"

"Yeah, you look nice, Pokie."

"What are you so scared of, anyway?"

"I'm not scared. I just don't want to sing in front

of lots of people."

"But you have a good singing voice," I said. "People will be disappointed if you don't sing."

"What if I forget the words?"

"You won't forget the words. You're just like all those famous actors I hear on TV. They're always talking about how nervous they get before they go onstage."

"Yeah?"

"Well, sure. Come on down from there. Your mother's all worried about you."

Junior swung his legs over and dropped to the ground. He was wearing a suit and a tie, and his tie was twisted up and around his collar.

"You look very grown up," I said. "Let me fix your tie here."

"Maybe you could walk me up to the school, huh, Pokie?"

I straightened his tie and brushed his jacket off. "Sure, I'll walk you up there. Someone has to make sure you go through with it."

He smiled, and the sun's reflection off his silvery metal railroad tracks nearly blinded me.

Sometimes I thought I was put on this Earth to look out for Junior Hollinger. I dragged him up to the junior high auditorium and stayed with him backstage until it was time for him to go on. Together we watched a skinny seventh-grade baton twirler, an off-key eighth-grade barbershop quartet, a roller-skating juggler, a very bad magician who tried to make his assistant disappear, only it didn't work, no matter how loud he screamed "ABRACADABRA!" Then came the girls' gymnastics team. One of them did a handspring and sprang herself right into the lap of a person in the front row of the audience.

"See?" I whispered to Junior. "You're a lot better than that magician or any of them."

Mrs. Schatz, my old English teacher, was running around backstage checking her clipboard and hurrying the acts on and off the stage. She walked over to Junior and me.

"Junior Hollinger, you're on next—Pokie? Is that you? I hardly recognized you. You've changed a lot since last year."

The gymnasts ran off the stage. Junior peeked around the curtain. "I changed my mind, Mrs. Schatz," he said. "*I'm* not going out there in front of all those people—"

Mrs. Schatz waved her clipboard in front of her like it was a fan. "Of *course* you're going out there! There's your music starting now."

Junior pulled on my arm. "You come with me, Pokie. I won't be so scared if you're out there with me—"

"Me! *You're* the one who wants to be in a talent show, not me!"

Mrs. Schatz looked like she might faint. Junior pulled me onstage. I could hear the introduction to "I Won't Grow Up" over the P.A. system. I could see that the auditorium was packed with proud parents and grandparents. Most of them had cameras hanging from their necks. Junior's face was full of animation as he sang and danced around me. I was so paralyzed I didn't even know when he'd finished singing. He had to grab me by the sleeve and drag me off the stage.

"Man, that was so cool, Pokie!" he said. "Listen to everyone clapping!"

"How could you *do* that to me!" I yelled.

"Maybe we could be a singing team, huh, Pokie?"

"Junior Hollinger, I've *had* it with you, do you understand? Not a day goes by that you don't drive me absolutely crazy!"

"If we went on tour, of course, you'd have to do a lot more than just stand there like you did today."

"You," I said, "are seriously warped."

April 30th

Dear Gib,

I'm through being Junior's keeper. I mean it. Today he dragged me up onstage during his talent show, and I stood there like an idiot while he sang and danced and brought the house down. I've decided that Junior is hazardous to my health, like cigarettes. He's a bad habit I'm giving up. I'm divorcing him as my friend. He's worried this means I won't come to his graduation and he's right.

I can't wait till you're home for summer and I have someone to talk to who's on *my* level. Someone to talk airplanes with. The other day I got out my *History of Aviation* book and some colored pencils. I drew a picture of a Boeing 747 and wished you were here to tell me if I got the wings right. I'll show it to you when you come home.

Love,
Pokie

May 6th

Dear Poke,

Don't be too hard on Junior. Sometimes he just can't help being Junior, and you shouldn't divorce him for that. He's been your friend for practically forever, Poke. He thinks a lot of you, and he'd be pretty upset if you skipped his graduation.

Got to run. I'm in a study group with some friends and we're getting ready for our finals. Won't be long till I'm home for summer. I can't wait!

Love,
Gib

It wasn't Gib's style to make me feel guilty about something, but his letter worked on my heart enough so that I took myself back to the school auditorium the first Friday in June. I sat and listened to the choir, heard the principal's speech, and watched Junior Hollinger collect his diploma.

When the ceremony was over, Junior and I decided to take our time and walk home the long way, while his parents went on ahead in the car. It was a beautiful, clear night. Junior stopped under every streetlight we came to and looked at his diploma.

"I never thought I'd graduate," he said. "I thought for a minute they might get me up onstage and tell everyone over the loudspeaker that I had to repeat the eighth grade."

I started laughing. "Did you really think they'd do that?"

"Well, sort of. My math grade was pretty bad this year. I never did get the hang of those equation things."

"You just don't have enough faith in yourself."

"Thanks for coming to my graduation, Pokie."

"I'm glad I came," I said. "Isn't it a beautiful night? Look at all the stars. . . ."

"Hey, Pokie, they got equations and stuff up there at the high school?"

"I can't believe you, Junior. . . . You just finished up one year of school and you're already worried about the next. I don't want to hear any more about school or grades! It's summer, Junior. You know what that means—"

"Swimming."

"Baseball."

"Bike riding."

"Ice cream."

"Yeah!" Junior said. "Summer!"

Part Three

19

"Looks like some people plan on sleeping the whole summer away."

It was Gib's voice. I was half in, half out of sleep.

I opened my eyes. Gib sat on the bed. It took me a second to figure things out: It was summer, and Gib was home.

Gib was home!

"Gib!" I threw my arms around him and gave him a hug. "I thought you weren't coming home till this afternoon."

"I caught an earlier flight. Come on downstairs, I'm making pancakes."

"Since when do you know how to make pancakes?"

"Since I decided to learn five minutes ago. Hurry up and get dressed," he said. "I need a human to test my pancakes on, and Mom and Dad have already left to do some shopping—"

"I'll be right down."

Gib was home. I jumped out of bed and pulled my clothes on and ran downstairs. Gib stood at the stove, pouring pancake batter into a skillet, and Junior sat at the kitchen table, a huge stack of pancakes in front of him.

"Couldn't believe it when Gib told me you weren't up yet," he said. "I just couldn't believe it."

I sat down at the table and looked at Gib. "What'd you let him in for? I thought you wanted to test your pancakes on someone *human*—"

"Har har, Pokie," Junior said. "Hey, Gib . . . you think you could put these in a Baggie for me to take home? I want to eat 'em while I watch Rocky and Bullwinkle."

"Why don't you just take the plate," Gib said. "You can bring it back later."

"Thanks!"

Junior poured a huge pool of syrup over his pancakes. He took his plate, his knife and fork, his napkin, and his glass of milk and bumped the screen door open with his backside and went home.

"Hell, he just moves in and takes over," I said.

Gib smiled and set a stack of pancakes in front of me. "He told me you went to his graduation. That was nice of you to do, Poke."

"Well, I wasn't going to, but your letter changed my mind." I took a bite of the pancakes. I was surprised. They were pretty good. "You sure you made these?"

"I had a little help," Gib said. He held up a box of Aunt Jemima Pancake Mix.

"I knew it!" I said.

Gib piled his plate high with pancakes and sat down and started in on them.

"I've got a few days before my summer job starts at Dog 'N' Suds," he said. "But until then, I think we should have some summer fun, don't you?"

"Yeah! What do you want to do?"

"Mitchell Field?"

"Really?"

"Sure."

"It's so neat having you back home," I said. "I really missed you, Gib."

"Let you in on a little secret," he said. "I missed you, too."

Gib remembered our Mitchell Field routine from last summer and parked right next to the "Do Not Enter—No Trespassing—Violators Will Be Prosecuted" sign.

"You still saving up for that flying lesson out

139

here, Gib?" I asked.

"I've been filling up my airplane bank all year," Gib said. "I should be able to afford it by the end of the summer."

"I've been saving my money too. I've got all my Christmas and birthday money in my coffee-can bank and my allowance, too. You think I should ask Mrs. Gregg down the street if I can baby-sit for her? That way, I could earn money twice as fast because she has twins—"

"You know what?" Gib said. "I think Junior is definitely affecting your brain."

I climbed up on the roof of the car and Gib sat on the hood.

"Hey, Gib . . . you think Mom and Dad'll let me take a flying lesson? They wouldn't let me go fishing out on that rowboat that time, remember?"

"You were pretty little then," Gib said. "I'll work on them this summer and talk them into it. Cessna 152 coming in for a landing."

I shielded my eyes from the sun and watched as the Cessna roared in over our heads for its landing.

"I'd like to have one like that," I said. "I want to fly jumbo jets for a living and have a little one like that for the weekends."

"Just so I can fly," Gib said. "That's all I care about."

The Cessna 152 rolled to a stop across the field, and Hank Jellies climbed out.

"Gib, look . . . wonder what happened to his Cherokee."

"It's in the hangar. I noticed it when we drove up."

Hank Jellies walked over to us. He wore a blue-and-gray plaid shirt and beat-up jeans.

"See, Gib? You can dress any way you want if you're a pilot."

"You'll be in a uniform when you fly those jumbo jets you're so crazy about—"

"That's different," I said. "I won't mind wearing a uniform if I'm flying to fancy places like New York or someplace."

"Hello there," Hank Jellies said. "Gib, right? And your sister Pokie. What do you think of the Cessna?"

"Is it yours?" I asked. I jumped down off the car. "How come you weren't flying the Cherokee?"

"The Cessna belongs to a friend of mine. He'll be flying it in the air show Saturday."

I looked at Gib. "Air show! You think we can come?"

"Sure, we'll be here," Gib said. "Is there going to be any stunt flying?"

Hank Jellies squinted in the sun. "Stunt flying, and we'll have lots of vintage aircraft. You two come on out Saturday and I'll introduce you around to some of the stunt pilots, okay?"

"Thanks," Gib said. "We'll be here."

Gib bought me an ice-cold Coke from the machine next to the airport office. We kicked off our shoes and sat on the grass and watched the planes come and go for most of the afternoon.

Some days are perfect ones, and this one was: Gib was beside me, and the whole summer lay ahead, wide and open, for us to fill any way we wanted.

20

"You got a postcard from your friend Lily," Junior said. "She's at camp. She's having a lot of fun riding horses and making centerpieces out of pinecones."

Junior stood at our screen door with a stack of mail in his hand.

"Who said you could go reading my mail before I do?" I said. I opened the door and snatched the mail out of his hand. I didn't bother with Lily's card since I already knew its contents. I looked through the rest of the letters.

"Gib got one from that girl of his," Junior said. "It smells like my ma's Lavoris."

I found the letter to Gib and smelled it; there

143

was a slight lavender scent to it.

"This isn't Lavoris," I said. "It's perfumed stationery. Don't you know anything?"

Gib came flying down the stairs. "Hi, Poke. Hi, Einstein."

"Einstein!" Junior said. "Pokie, did you hear that? Gib called me Einstein!"

"I heard," I said. "Gib, you really should watch how you talk to Junior. You know the least little thing sets him off into a laughing fit—"

"Any mail for me?"

"You got a letter from your girl," Junior said. "I think she wrote it while she was gargling with her mouthwash."

Gib grinned and took the letter from me and went into the kitchen.

"Einstein!" Junior said. "Man, is that ever funny! Hey, Pokie?"

"What?"

"Who's Einstein?"

"Lord!" I said.

Gib started work at Dog 'N' Suds Friday afternoon. While he was gone I started getting ready for the air show the next day. I crawled around the attic and found my binoculars and thermos, my sketch pad and colored pencils. I loaded up my Kodak and packed everything into a giant tote bag. I couldn't wait to show Gib my air-show supplies. I was sitting out on the front steps, ready for

144

him when he got home from work.

"Hey there," he said, and dropped a small sack into my lap.

"What is it?"

"One of those foot-longs from Dog 'N' Suds."

"Thanks. . . . Look what I packed for the air show, Gib." I held the tote bag open and showed everything to him. "I've got my camera in there and my sketch pad so I can draw some of those antique airplanes—"

"Oh . . . Poke . . ." Gib's voice sounded flat. He sat down next to me. "I don't exactly know how to tell you this, but I don't think we can go to the air show tomorrow—"

I looked at him hard. "What do you mean?"

"Nell's coming. Didn't Mom tell you?"

"Nell? She's coming here?"

"For a visit. I can't wait for you to meet her."

"When's she coming?"

"Around noon tomorrow."

I stared straight ahead. "Nobody tells me anything."

"Well, I didn't know, either. Not till she called me this morning. I guess you weren't up yet."

"Oh. Here." I handed him the sack with the foot-long hot dog in it. "I'm not hungry."

"I'm going down to the train station and pick her up on my lunch hour tomorrow. You want to come with me?"

"I don't know. I might be busy with something."

145

"I'm sorry about the air show, Poke. Listen—maybe the three of us can go out to the airfield sometime next week, huh? You, Nell, and me."

"Yeah," I said. "Maybe."

So Nell was coming for a visit, and the next morning I got kicked out of my room.

"Where am *I* supposed to sleep?" I asked my mother. She was yanking the sheets off my bed.

"In Gib's room, and Gib will sleep on a cot in the family room."

"Why can't Nell sleep in Gib's room?"

"Because she's a guest and no guest wants to sleep in a room that looks like O'Hare Airport."

My mother bundled the pillowcases and sheets together and handed them to me. "Run downstairs and put those in the washer. Then go outside and try to find some pretty flowers. We'll put them in a vase here on your dresser. Lord," she said, looking around, "this room could really use a coat of paint."

"Pokie!" Gib hollered from downstairs. "Junior Hollinger's here."

"Tell him I'm not home!" I yelled.

"I know you're up there, Pokie," Junior said. "Come on down and I'll show you my new pack of baseball cards—"

"I don't care about your baseball cards!"

My mother frowned. "You go on downstairs and stop being so rude to Junior. Go on now."

I took the bundle of sheets down some of the stairs and stood on the landing. "Here," I said. "Catch." I tossed the sheets to Junior. "You can help me wash those—we're having company."

"What company?"

"Gib's girlfriend." We went down to the basement. I found the box of Tide and handed it to Junior. "Put a couple of handfuls in," I said. "What kind of cards you got?"

"Cubs."

"Yeah? You chew the gum?"

"Here." He reached into his back pocket and pulled out the baseball cards. I found the pink square of gum, bit off a piece, and gave him the rest. "Gib's girl is coming, huh?"

"She's coming all the way from Independence just to see him."

He stuffed the sheets in the washer and dumped the Tide in; then we sat on the cement floor and looked through the baseball cards.

"You can keep André Dawson if you want," Junior said. "I got two of him."

"Junior . . . you never got yourself a crush on some girl, did you?"

"Sure. Lots of times."

"Yeah? A crush is different than love, though, right? A crush is one-sided. In real love there's two people and some sort of chemical reaction."

"Like photosynthesis."

I burst out laughing. "Photosynthesis!"

Junior's face got red. "Well, maybe not *exactly* like photosynthesis."

"That's with plants. You'll learn about it this year in the ninth grade." I patted his hand. "Sorry I laughed."

He shrugged and blew a big pink bubble out of the gum. "Pokie . . . you want to take me up there to the high school and show me around? If I know where all the classrooms are I might not be so nervous the first day—"

"I swear, I just can't believe you sometimes! Remember all that stuff you told me about the high school last year? You got me scared to death! And now you expect me to take you on a guided tour?"

"Come on, Pokie. I was just having fun when I told you that stuff. You knew I was kidding, didn't you?"

"No," I said. "Anyway, I can't take you on a tour today. Gib wants me to go with him down to the station to meet Nell."

"Well, maybe tomorrow then, huh?"

"Maybe." I stretched my legs out in front of me. "I wonder if this girl's really in love with Gib, or if she's just got a crush on him."

"Missouri's a long way to travel from just for a crush."

"Yeah," I said. "Yeah . . . she must really like him."

148

21

Nell was nothing like I expected. For some reason I pictured Nell looking like the girl who was crowned Miss Lilac at last year's flower festival: a tall girl with a golden tan and lots of curves. But when Nell stepped off the train I saw a pale slip of a girl even shorter than me, a girl who wore a goofy yellow sundress with no straps. Every time it looked like the dress was going to slide down and leave her naked on top, she'd give it a yank up to her neck.

"Gib!" She ran to Gib, and they stood there and kissed in the middle of all the commuters. They kissed like they had practiced kissing many times before.

After a long time Gib managed to regain some of his senses and untangle himself from Nell.

"I want you to meet someone," he said. He took her hand and brought her over to me. "Nell, this is Pokie."

Nell smiled. "Hi, Pokie. It's really nice to meet you."

"Hi," I said.

"Is this all the luggage you have?" Gib asked. He picked up Nell's suitcase, and they walked ahead of me, holding hands.

"I didn't take time to pack anything more," Nell said. "I just wanted to get out of there." She looked over her shoulder at me. "I had a fight with my parents."

"And you ran away?" I asked.

She laughed. "No. They know where I am, all right."

"Oh."

"They still giving you a hard time about us?" Gib said.

"Oh, the same old thing. You know. 'Nell, you're much too young to get so serious over some boy. Nell, you're going to flunk out of college if you don't stop mooning over some boy. Nell, you can't go visit some boy unless his parents invite you.'"

"Heck, you know how parents are," Gib said. "You'd think they were never our age." He put his arm around Nell and pulled her close, and on the

150

way to the car they talked in such low voices I couldn't hear a thing they said.

My mother threw her arms around Nell as soon as she walked into the house. My mother is very good at making strangers and stray animals feel welcome. She took Nell's hand and led her into the living room and introduced her to my father.

"We're so glad you could spend some time with us," my mother said. "Are you tired from your long trip? Gib will show you to your room if you'd like to rest before dinner."

"Oh, that'd be great," she said. "Honestly, you must think I'm just awful, barging in on you like this—"

"Not at all," my mother said.

Gib picked up Nell's suitcase. "C'mon, hon. I'll take you upstairs. You're staying in Pokie's room."

"I don't want to put anyone out," Nell said, and there was this long pause where I was supposed to say, "Oh, you're not putting me out at all," only I didn't say it.

"Pokie is delighted you're staying in her room," my mother said, and Nell smiled.

As soon as they were gone my mother and father looked at each other.

"Well?" I said. "I can't tell you how shocked I was when she got off the train wearing a nudist's dress."

My father grinned. "What do you think, Pokie? You think Gib's head over heels in love with this girl?"

"I don't exactly think it's love," I said. "I think it's just a chemical reaction. Like photosynthesis."

22

Nell and Gib held hands all during dinner. I didn't see how they were going to manage eating, but Gib switched to his left hand and ate his meat loaf that way.

"You're from Independence, is that right?" Kate asked.

"Yes," Nell said. "Where Harry Truman grew up."

"We got some important people who grew up right here," I said. "You ever hear of Adrian Diffendaffer? He invented squeakless chalk so teachers wouldn't hurt their ears when they wrote on the blackboard."

"Poke, where'd you hear that story?" Gib said. "Junior Hollinger, I'll bet."

I frowned. "It's not a story."

Gib looked at Nell. "Junior Hollinger's Pokie's little friend. He's always telling her some wild story."

"He is not my *little* friend," I said. "He grew three inches since last summer."

Nell smiled. "Is he sweet on you?"

"Junior? Hell, no! He just likes to torment me is all."

My mother cleared her throat. "Nell? What courses are you taking at school?"

"Oh, criminal justice and European history. My favorite class is political science, though, because that's where I met Gib."

Gib grinned and squeezed Nell's hand. "I was sitting there in poli. sci., listening to a boring lecture, when the door opened and Nell ran in— twenty minutes late and out of breath."

"The campus is so big I just couldn't find the right lecture hall," Nell said.

I shook my head. "In *our* school you get an automatic detention if you're even a *minute* late."

"Anyway," Gib said, "she sat down next to me and asked if she could borrow a pen and some paper—"

"Well, you wouldn't last a second with my Latin teacher, Miss Leffingwell," I said. "If you don't bring your notebook and pen every day she makes you write 'I will come to class prepared' a hundred times. In Latin!"

"College is different," Gib said. "They treat us like adults there, not children."

"I'm not children!" I said. "I most certainly am not children! I'm fourteen and—"

"Pokie," my mother said. "Would you please bring out the rest of the meat loaf? It looks like some of these folks would like seconds."

My mother didn't look too happy, so I decided to keep my mouth shut and get the meat loaf. I had to sit there through the rest of dinner and watch Gib and Nell stare into each other's eyes and do a lot of giggling. They acted like they were the only two people on Earth and I was the Invisible Man.

After dinner Kate and my mother and father cleared the table while Nell and Gib went outside to the porch. I figured the outside belonged to everyone, so I sort of followed them.

"Pokie," my mother said. "We can use your help here."

I looked at her. "Four people to clear the table?"

"Yes," she said. So I picked up a cup and a saucer and took them out to the kitchen. My mother put her hand on my shoulder. "I think Nell and Gib should have some time alone, don't you?"

"I wasn't going to bother them," I said.

"You stay out of their way tonight, all right? Here." She handed me a stack of dishes, and I started loading them into the dishwasher.

Kate attacked the leftovers with a roll of Saran Wrap. "Nell seems like a nice girl," she said. "They remind me of you two when you were courting."

"What's courting?" I asked.

"Courting," my father said, pinching my nose. "Sparking. Dating."

"Oh. Well, what he sees in her is beyond me," I said. "For one thing, she doesn't have any meat on her bones. And for another, she doesn't carry any paper or pens with her."

Kate and my mother and father all started laughing. I stood up straight and put my hands on my hips.

"What's so *funny?*" I asked.

"You," my father said. "You're pretty cute, you know that?"

"Yeah," I said. "I know it."

That night, for the first time in a long time I had my treehouse dream. I felt myself tripping on the rickety platform and tumbling over and over in space. I woke as I hit the ground. I jumped out of bed and went looking for Gib. The house was dark; I made my way downstairs and heard Gib and Nell outside on the porch swing. They were talking quietly, almost in whispers. I didn't want Nell to know my problems, but I needed to talk to Gib. I opened the screen door and stepped out onto the porch.

"Gib?"

"Poke . . . what are you doing up?"

"I have to talk to you about something."

"What?"

"It's private."

Gib pushed himself up from the swing and its hinges creaked. He walked over to me. "What is it, Poke? You should be in bed. . . ."

"I had that bad dream again," I whispered. "The one where I'm falling out of the tree-house—"

"Oh . . . Poke, look, you'll be okay. It was just a dream."

"Could you read to me like you did the other time?"

"What's wrong?" I heard Nell say. "Is there anything I can help with?"

"No, it's okay," Gib said. He put his arm around my shoulders and walked me inside. "Pokie, look . . . you'll be all right. You can read to yourself."

He went back outside and the swing hinges squeaked and the talking started up again. Love talk, quiet and low. I turned around and ran upstairs and got into bed. I didn't sleep for a long time. Gib had forgotten what night terrors were like. He had forgotten how to be a good brother. He had forgotten me.

23

Nell slept till noon the next day. I didn't think that was quite right; after all, I never heard of someone pounding her ear till noon while her true love went off to grill wienies at the Dog 'N' Suds. When she finally got up she came padding down the hall in a short little nightie with lace on the bottom.

"I never saw pajamas like that before," I said.

"Well, hi," she said. "Did you finally get to sleep last night? Gib said you had a bad dream."

"Yeah, I got to sleep."

"Good."

She shut the bathroom door. After a minute or so I said, "You always sleep this late at home?"

"Gib and I stayed up pretty late," she said. "We talked till almost two."

"What'd you talk about?"

"Oh, lots of things." She opened the door. "Your brother's very romantic, you know."

"Gib?"

"He writes me poetry, right out of his head. How about that? Bet you didn't know your brother was a poet now, did you?"

"No. He almost flunked English in the tenth grade."

"Well, I guess he's improved a lot since then, huh?"

"He's more interested in airplanes than he is in poetry. Have you seen his room yet?"

"Not yet."

I took her down the hall to Gib's room and opened the door. Her eyes got very wide when she saw all the airplanes.

"*Look* at all this," she said.

I pointed to one of the planes hanging from the ceiling. "Know what that is? It's an A-20 from World War II. And the one next to it is a Curtis-Jenny biplane from World War I."

"You sure know a lot about airplanes," Nell said.

"Gib thought maybe the three of us could go out to the airfield and watch the planes land while you're here. Want to?"

"Well, sure."

"As soon as he gets home, okay?"

"Sure," Nell said. "Fine."

That afternoon Junior pitched to me while I spun around and tried to hit the ball.

"You know this is a lost cause, Pokie," he said. "We do this every summer. I pitch and you miss. The only time you ever hit it is when Gib helps you."

"Just throw the ball, Junior."

Junior sighed deeply and pitched the ball. I swung the bat, and somehow the ball ended up behind me.

"See?" Junior said. "Can't we play something you're *good* at?"

Suddenly Nell appeared around the corner of the house. "Hi," she said. She was wearing a University of Missouri T-shirt and cut-off jeans. "I'm Nell," she said to Junior.

Junior stuck his hand out like he was in a business meeting. "Junior Hollinger," he said. "I like the way your letter to Gib smelled."

Nell laughed. She ran her fingers through her hair. "I used to play baseball all the time. A group of kids on my block had a pretty good team."

"No kidding?" Junior said. "Get out of the way, Pokie. I want to pitch one to Nell."

I glared at him. "Nell doesn't want to play with us—"

"No, I'd love to," she said. She picked up the ball

161

and tossed it to Junior.

"Give her the bat, Pokie," Junior said.

I held the bat out to Nell. "Better stand back," she said. So I stood back. It wasn't enough to get kicked out of my room; now I was getting kicked out of my own baseball practice.

Nell held the bat over her shoulder. Junior took a step back and let loose with one of his power pitches. Nell whacked the ball clear over the maple tree at the far end of the yard.

"Man! Look at it go!" Junior yelled. "Did you *see* that, Pokie?"

"For God's sake, of *course* I saw it!"

A car horn beeped out in our driveway. "Bet Gib's home," Nell said. She smiled and handed the bat to me and ran off.

"I'm gonna get *me* a girl like that when I'm older," Junior said. "Someone with pretty legs who can hit a baseball."

"Anybody can get lucky and hit a ball one time," I said.

"Yeah, anybody but you, Pokie."

I frowned. "Why don't you just take your bat and go home and watch Rocky and Bullwinkle?"

"Holy cow, I almost forgot! Thanks, Pokie."

Junior was in love with Rocky and Bullwinkle, and Gib was in love with Nell. I was between those two stages. I was at the middle stage, where I wasn't in love with a person or with a cartoon.

It was a hard place to be.

24

"Gib, are you sure you should park here?" Nell asked. "It says 'No Trespassing.'"

"Shoot, Gib and I always park here," I said. "Nothing ever happens. Come on." I got out of the car and scrambled up on the roof. I watched some of the small planes circling the field.

"Wow, it's really loud!" Nell said.

"A little noise never hurt anyone," I shouted. "Gib, look! Beech Bonanza taking off right over us!"

I couldn't hear Gib's answer over the Bonanza's engines. I watched the sky for a long time and pretended Gib and I were up there in our own planes, waiting for an okay to land.

"Gib?" I yelled. "Look down the runway! Piper Cherokee coming in for a landing! Maybe it's Hank Jellies. . . . Gib?"

It occurred to me that I hadn't heard from Gib and Nell in a while. I jumped down from the roof of the car and looked around. Gib and Nell had disappeared. I walked beside the airfield fence, peeked into the airplane hangars, walked back to the car. It played in my mind that something had happened to Gib and Nell—like maybe they'd been kidnapped by an insane airplane mechanic and forced to fly to Nebraska or someplace. I leaned against the car and tried to look not worried.

The Piper Cherokee taxied to a stop not far from me and Hank Jellies climbed out. "Hello, there . . ."

"Hi . . . um, you see my brother when you were flying around up there? He's with his girl and she's wearing a University of Missouri T-shirt and cut-off jeans."

Hank Jellies nodded over toward a field of tall grass, and sure enough, there were Gib and Nell; sitting in the middle of that field, kissing each other.

"Oh," I said. "He's supposed to be watching the airplanes land."

"If I were his age I think I'd rather sit in a field with a pretty girl than watch airplanes land." He leaned against the fence and looked at me. "Didn't

164

see you two at the air show. . . ."

"We had to meet my brother's girlfriend at the train station, so we couldn't come."

"Listen, one of my students canceled her lesson, so I've got a free hour this afternoon. Think you and your brother might like to take a ride in the Cherokee?"

My heart stopped, it really did. "When? Now, you mean?"

Hank Jellies nodded. "Why don't you go find out if he's interested. I'll be in the airport office, having my coffee break."

"Okay. Thanks!"

I ran across the grassy field. Gib held Nell's hands and pulled her to her feet, then he helped her brush the grass off her cut-offs.

"Poke, I was just coming to get you. . . . Would you mind if we went home now? Nell and I want to go into the city and do some sightseeing—"

"I've never seen Chicago before," Nell said. "Except to change trains—"

"But Gib," I said, "I just saw Hank Jellies, and he wants to take us up in his Cherokee. It has to be right now. One of his students canceled her lesson."

Gib and Nell looked at each other, then Gib looked at me.

"Poke, I made reservations at a nice restaurant for Nell and me, and we'll be late if we don't catch the four forty into the city—"

165

"Oh . . ."

"Why don't you go ahead and go?" Gib said. "I'll tell Mom and Dad, and they'll pick you up—"

"No," I said. "It wouldn't be any fun without you."

On the way home Nell scrunched around in the front seat and looked at me. "I'm sorry about your airplane ride, Pokie. Maybe you and Gib can do it some other time."

"Probably won't ever get another chance like this again," I said. "Not unless we pay for it, and it costs seventy-five dollars to go up for a lesson—"

"Come on, Poke," Gib said. "You're being pretty dramatic—"

"Never thought I'd see the day when you'd rather go to some *restaurant* than get a free ride in a Piper Cherokee—"

"It's just that Nell and I want to spend some time together," he said. "You can understand that, can't you?"

What could I say to that? I leaned back and watched the sky out the rear window. I pretended I was up there in my Piper Cherokee, doing my first solo flight, flying low and circling twice.

Twice. So Gib would notice me.

25

Junior invited me to a picnic a few days later. We sat in the backyard under the maple tree and ate peanut butter and honey sandwiches and drank milk straight from the carton.

"How much time they give you up there at the high school for changing classes?" he asked.

"Five minutes," I said. "Are you still worried about high school? It's easy. You'll get the hang of it in no time."

"But remember that time you told me about when you got lost and walked into the boys' locker room by mistake? What if that happens to me?"

"Well, there won't be any problem if it happens

to you, Junior, because you're a boy."

"No, Pokie, you know what I mean. What if I get lost and end up in the wrong place?"

"Everybody gets lost the first day or so. The teachers understand that."

"I seen Gib's girl this morning," Junior said. "She came outside in her nightie and stuck a post-card in the mailbox for the mailman to take."

"She's awful the way she parades around in her night things," I said. "It's illegal to go outside in your nightie, isn't it?"

"Where'd you hear that?"

"I don't know. Somewhere." I gulped down the last swallow of milk from the carton. "I tell you about that pilot out at Mitchell offering me a free ride in his airplane?"

"Only about a million times, Pokie."

I gave him a dirty look. "Well, I don't mean to keep talking about it. It's just that I'm so used to talking to Gib about flying, and now he's too busy with Nell to listen to me."

"Well, why don't you take that lesson yourself? You've got enough saved up, don't you?"

"Almost . . . but I always pictured Gib and me doing it together. . . . I mean, taking a flying lesson won't be much fun if I don't have Gib to share it with."

"When's Gib's girl leaving?"

"I don't know. She's been here a week and I'm already sick of her."

"Well, I like her, Pokie."

"You like her!"

"It's a free country. I can like her if I want."

"You just like her because she can hit a base-ball."

"No, Pokie, it's got nothing to do with baseball. There's some people you meet and you like 'em right off the bat. Hey, Pokie! Right off the bat! Like baseball! Get it?"

"I get it!" I said. "Good grief . . ."

"Hi!" Nell called. She walked across the yard to Junior and me. "You two having a picnic?"

"You want to join us?" Junior asked, and I elbowed him in the ribs so hard he made a noise like *Oooff!*

"Well, I just came to tell Pokie that her mom and I are going out shopping for a while. Either of you want to come along?"

"No, we got some things to do," I said.

Junior looked at me, confused. "What things?"

"Just *things*," I said.

"Well," Nell said, "we'll see you later, then. 'Bye."

"Yeah," Junior said. "'Bye!"

We watched her walk away.

"She's really pretty, isn't she, Pokie?"

"I don't think she's so pretty."

"How come you don't wear makeup like she does?"

"Because I don't need it!" I said. "You should

169

see her without her makeup. She's a completely different-looking girl. Very homely."

"What's homely?"

"Ugly!"

"I like the way she wears that blue stuff on her eyelids."

I crammed the last bit of sandwich in my mouth and stood up. "Come on. I'm going to get that postcard out of the mailbox and see what she wrote on it. Maybe she wrote her parents and told them when she's coming home."

"You can't read her mail, Pokie. It's against the law."

"Against the law! You read my mail anytime you can get your hands on it!"

"Oh, yeah," Junior said. "You aren't going to call the police, are you, Pokie?"

"Lord! Come on. . . ."

We ran up to the front porch, and I reached into the mailbox and pulled out Nell's postcard. On the front was a picture of a field, with fancy red letters across the bottom that said:

GREETINGS FROM ILLINOIS—

THE PRAIRIE STATE

I turned it over and read the back:

Dear Mama and Daddy,

I'm sorry about the fight we had before I left, but I'm 19 now, old enough to know what I'm doing. Gib's a wonderful boy—you said so yourselves when he visited at Christmas—so I don't see what you're so worried about.

I don't know exactly when I'll be home. I'll call you at the end of the week and let you know my plans.

Love,
Nell

Mick and Dolly Potts
903 W. Waldo
Independence, Mo.
64051

"Look at this!" I said. "She's going to be here forever!"

"You mean she's going to live here from now on?" Junior asked.

"Lord, I hope not!"

"Well, maybe she and Gib will have a fight and she'll go home sooner."

"You haven't seen them together. They do the opposite of fighting."

"What's that?"

"Oh, brother," I said. "Sometimes I forget how young you are." I shoved the postcard back in the mailbox. "Come on."

"Where to?"

"I don't know. Just come on." I started walking quickly down Kenilworth, and Junior followed me. "Nell's very bad for Gib. She sleeps late while he has to go out to work."

"But how is it bad for him if she sleeps while

he's working?"

"Well, for God's sake, it shows how different they are! He's a hard worker and she's lazy! You wouldn't want your girlfriend to be lazy, would you?"

"I wouldn't mind," Junior said.

"I don't know why I try to have a serious conversation with you. You miss the point every time."

We walked to town. Junior had to step on every crack he came to.

"Sometimes I feel like I'm with a two-year-old when you do things like that," I said.

"Used to be you liked stepping on cracks with me," Junior said.

"I just don't get anything from it anymore," I said, and Junior stopped stepping on cracks and started walking regular. "We're not too far from Dog 'N' Suds. Let's stop by and see if we can get a couple of free hot dogs from Gib."

"If we go down Hawthorne we could stop by the high school. You could show me around a little."

"Look, Junior. If I hear any more about the high school from you, I'll spit up. I mean it."

Junior got a pinched look on his face. "You only think of yourself since you're fourteen. I think you're a very selfish person. I don't want any free hot dogs. I'm going home."

I felt a sudden pain in my stomach. "Well, fine!

Go home—you . . . you . . . thirteen-year-old!"

He turned around to go, then turned back to me and said quietly, "You know something, Pokie . . . you're jealous of Gib's girl."

"Jealous! Jealous of *Nell*?"

"You heard me." He started walking away from me.

I saw lights I was so mad. I wanted to murder him.

"Junior Hollinger, you come back here!" I hollered, but he just kept on walking. "Why would I be jealous of someone who's *shorter* than me!"

Junior kept on walking. I turned around and ran to town. Down Main Street and up Park. I ran all the way to Dog 'N' Suds. Gib was working at the take-out window. I had to stand in line behind five people before I got a chance to talk to him.

"Well, look who's here," he said. "What'll it be?"

"I don't know. A cheese dog, I guess. And a root beer."

I watched Gib split a hot dog, fill it with cheese, and put it on the grill. "What's wrong?" he said. "You're mad at something—I can tell."

"I'm not mad. I've just got a lot of things on my mind is all."

He filled a tall glass from the root-beer dispenser and set it down in front of me.

"I think maybe you should have a talk with Nell," I said. "People have been telling me she's

173

running around the neighborhood in her nightie."

Gib laughed. "What people? Junior Hollinger, you mean."

I studied my root beer for a minute. "Don't you care about flying anymore?"

"What? Sure, I do. Why?"

"I don't know. I just thought you'd given up the idea about becoming a pilot."

"Hell, no. What made you think that? I still want to take that introductory flying lesson." He spread a bun with butter and dropped it onto the grill. "I can see you now . . . sitting there on the roof of the car while I take off. I'll get Hank Jellies to let me circle twice, like we always talk about—"

"Maybe *I'll* be the one doing the circling," I said. I felt a whole lot of things cramping my heart, things I had to get out. "You keep forgetting that maybe I get tired of you doing everything exciting and me just watching!"

Gib looked surprised. "What do *I* do that's so exciting? I work and go to college—things you'll probably be doing yourself before too long."

"You don't understand," I said. I fooled around with the straw in my root-beer glass. "You and me . . . we used to do things together and now you're leaving me behind."

He squinted and looked at me hard. "I'm not leaving you behind, Poke. I'm just getting older. Growing up. Like you are."

174

"Me? *I'm* not the one who's growing up."

"Well, I reckon you haven't looked in the mirror lately," he said. "Because you're growing up faster than anyone."

I didn't say anything. Gib took my hot dog off the grill and wrapped it in paper and handed it to me.

I used to love cheese dogs, but not this one. It was cooked all right, but, I don't know—it just sort of stuck in my throat going down.

26

"Where's Junior Hollinger keeping himself these days?" my mother asked. "I haven't seen him around lately."

"I don't know where he is and I don't care."

I was sitting on the porch swing with my legs stuck out in front of me and my feet hooked over the porch railing.

"You two have a fight?"

"Junior's enough to make an angel swear," I said. "He just riles me all the time now."

"We're having a neighborhood cookout this weekend. Think maybe you should invite him?"

"No."

"I see," my mother said. She sat down next to

me and stretched her legs out like mine and hooked her feet over the porch railing.

"How long is Nell going to be here?" I asked.

"I don't know. She hasn't said anything, but I don't think she gets along too well with her parents. I'm not sure she's anxious to go home."

"Well, she's been here over two weeks! If she doesn't go home soon, you and Dad'll have to adopt her!"

My mother laughed. "Nell's very easy to have as a guest. . . . She helps around the house and she's fun to do things with. I wish you'd come along the day we went shopping. We had a lot of fun."

"I wish it were last summer," I said. "Last summer I had Gib all to myself."

"Gib's making a life of his own now. Just like you'll do someday."

Kate walked across the front yard. She carried a china mug in one hand and her shoes in the other. "How can you ladies have a coffee klatch without coffee?"

"We're not klatching," my mother said. "We're discussing what happens to sisters when brothers grow up."

"Ah," Kate said. "The theory of relativity." She walked up the porch steps and sat down on the swing. She stuck her legs out like we had ours. "Saw Junior Hollinger a few minutes ago spinning around on that tire swing of his. He looked mighty lonely."

"Now, don't you start on that, Kate," I said. "I just got through telling Mom that Junior and I are finished. You two don't know how he can get on my nerves sometimes."

"Oh, I think we can imagine how Junior can get on someone's nerves," Kate said, and I smiled a little.

The screen door opened and Nell walked out onto the porch. She had knobby hair curlers all over her head, and she was carrying a bottle of pink nail polish. "Is there room for one more?"

"Climb aboard," Kate said, and Nell sat down and hooked her ankles over the railing like the rest of us. She started painting her fingernails. I had come out to the porch to be alone and here I was, in the middle of a crowd.

"You should have seen Gib and me earlier," Nell said. "He was talking to me about airplanes, and it got me to wondering: Just how does an airplane stay up in the air? I can understand how a car goes, and even a train, but this flying business escapes me. So Gib tried to demonstrate by taking the airplane bank you made, Pokie, and running around the room with it like he was a kid!"

Kate and my mother laughed, but I didn't. The idea of Gib teaching Nell anything about flying really made my blood boil.

"Shoot, don't you know anything about aerodynamics?" I said. "Drag's generated from lift, and that creates flight. Simple!"

Nell held her fingers out in front of her, and I could see her nails, shiny pink from the wet polish.

"Maybe you could teach me a little about airplanes," Nell said. "Gib's so wild about them, and I never know what the Sam Hill he's talking about—"

"I don't have time to be teaching any beginner about airplanes," I said. "I have a lot of things to do. I have to write my friend Lily at camp. She's studying pinecone art."

I didn't look at my mother, but I could feel her looking at me. It felt uncomfortable. How she could make me feel that way with just her eyeballs was something I'd never been able to figure out.

"I need someone to go shopping for our cookout this weekend," my mother said. "Are there any volunteers?"

"I'd love to shop for you," Nell said. "Just tell me what to get."

"I'll make a list out for you. Pokie will go with you and help."

"*What?*" I said.

"You can put off writing that postcard for a little while, can't you?" she asked.

The way she said it meant I didn't have a choice. I was being forced to go to the grocery store with Nell.

Nell blew on her fingernails. "When do you want to go, Pokie?"

I glanced at my mother. Her left eyebrow was raised.

"I don't know," I said. "Whenever you're ready, I guess."

Nell got herself all dolled up for the grocery store: She French braided her hair and put on wire loop earrings, and she wore a white sweater and slacks outfit. I felt very grubby walking up and down the aisles next to her: I noticed I had a tomato-juice stain on my T-shirt, and my hair was sticking out funny from being out in the heat and humidity.

"Let's see," Nell said. "We've got the hot dogs, the hamburger, the buns . . . what's next?"

I looked at the grocery list and tried to decipher my mother's handwriting. "Potato chips."

"Potato chips . . . which way?"

"Aisle three."

Nell made a U-turn and we headed for the potato-chip aisle. I grabbed a big bag of Ruffles and tossed it into the basket.

"We have to get a watermelon, too," I said. "Aisle one."

We wheeled over to the produce section. Nell went around thumping watermelons till she found just the right one.

"This seems like a nice ripe one," she said.

"Where'd you learn to do that?"

"Tell if a melon's ripe? My mama, I guess . . . she's a real expert at picking out just the right fruits and vegetables."

"Don't you think you should go home?" I said. "Maybe your parents are having a cookout of their own."

"I just don't see eye to eye with my parents these days," she said. She put the melon in the shopping cart and we started for the checkout line. "I mean, I love them and everything, but we seem to argue all the time now."

"How come? Because of Gib?"

"They didn't want me getting serious about a boy until I finished college. . . . That was my plan, too. Before I met Gib."

We paid for the groceries and carried them out to the car. It was a shock to go from the air-conditioned store into the suffocating summer heat outside.

"Almost as hot and humid as it is in Missouri," Nell said. "Do you like ice cream?"

"Yeah," I said. "Yeah, I like ice cream."

"Point me in the direction of an ice cream place."

I took her to Webb's, a drugstore with an old-fashioned soda fountain. We sat at the curved marble counter and ate two chocolate-fudge double-dipped cones with sprinkles.

"When I'm hot like this, only thing cools me off is ice cream," Nell said. "Pokie? You know, I didn't set out to fall in love. I met Gib and it just happened—"

"I don't want to hear about any of that stuff," I said.

She put her hand on my arm. "But I want you to listen to it. You've got to understand something, Pokie. What you and Gib have . . . nothing's going to change that."

I felt my face get hot. I looked away from Nell and concentrated on my ice cream cone. I didn't know what to say, so I didn't say anything. We finished our ice cream cones, and Nell put some money on the counter.

"You ready to go?" she asked.

"Yeah," I said. I glanced over at her. "Nell? You think you could show me how to do up my hair in a French braid like that?"

She smiled. "Sure," she said. "It's easy. It just takes a little patience is all."

27

Nell French braided my hair for our neighborhood cookout. She sat on my bed and I sat in front of her on the floor while she pulled my hair up and braided it under.

"When I was in high school my girlfriends and I used to do each other's hair all the time," she said. "One time my friend and I bought a drugstore kit to highlight our hair, and we ended up with these awful-looking orange stripes in it."

"What'd you do?" I asked.

"We put big scarves on our heads and went down to the Cut and Curl—that's a beauty parlor—and they worked on us a whole afternoon to straighten it out."

"I never thought about dying my hair," I said. "I don't think my mother would like it very well if I did."

"You don't have to, Pokie. Your hair's already a pretty color. It's just like Gib's." She fastened my hair with an elastic band. "There you go. . . . I'll get you a mirror so you can see it from the back."

Nell gave me her compact, and I held it up so I could see the back of my head in the dresser mirror.

"My friend Lily's good at curling hair," I said. "But I don't think she can do a French braid."

"Whoa!" I heard Gib say. "Who's the movie star?"

I turned around and looked at Gib standing in my doorway. "Come on, Gib . . . cut it out."

"Hot stuff, Poke. Very hot stuff."

Nell smiled. "Stop it, Gib. You're embarrassing her."

"You girls better get a move on if you want anything to eat. We've already got a crowd."

"We'll be right down," Nell said. Gib went off down the hall. "You've got some wisps of hair sticking out a little," she said. She picked up a can of hairspray. "Shut your eyes for a second."

I squeezed my eyes shut, and Nell sprayed a cloud of hairspray around my braid. I could feel her tucking little strands of hair into the braid. She had a very light touch.

"There," she said. "Perfect."

Gib was in charge of the grill at our cookout.

"This is as bad as working at Dog 'N' Suds," he said. "You like your hamburger well done, don't you, Poke?"

"I like it burned on the outside," I said.

Our backyard was plenty jammed: Every lawn chair was occupied, and the picnic table was crowded with more people than it was ever intended for. Latecomers sat cross-legged on the grass eating their hot dogs and hamburgers. I saw Kate introducing Nell around to some of the neighbors. I saw Junior's parents, but I didn't see Junior. It wasn't like him to stay away from a cookout, even if we *were* divorced.

"He was asking about you this morning," Gib said.

"Who was?"

"You know who. Junior."

"Oh," I said. "Him."

"Mom called and invited the Hollingers over, but Junior wouldn't come."

"Junior's very weird these days. I can't figure him out."

"You two on the outs?"

"We're not on the outs," I said. "We're not on the outs at all. It's just that he's a child, and I can't stand all those child ways of his."

"He's only a year younger than you, Poke."

"But I've outgrown him, Gib. I can't help it. I've

just outgrown him."

"Yeah," he said. "I know." He slid my hamburger onto a bun and fixed it up just the way I like it, with double doses of ketchup and onions.

I spotted my parents sitting on the grass near our maple tree. I walked over to them and modeled my new hairdo.

"How do you like it?" I asked. I turned around so they could see it from the back. "Nell did it. It's called a French braid."

"Pretty nifty," my father said. "Makes you look like those models on the magazine covers."

I started in on my hamburger. In a little while Kate drifted over, then Gib and Nell.

"These are the last of the hamburgers," Gib said. "If anyone else comes, they're out of luck."

"I didn't think we'd have quite this many," my mother said. "Guess everyone came because they heard we had a professional cook in the family."

Gib laughed. "Just for the summers. I don't plan on working at Dog 'N' Suds for the rest of my life."

Nell looked over at Gib and brushed some hair out of his eyes. "A pilot someday." She turned and looked at me. "Maybe two."

"Someday," I said.

28

The next Saturday after I collected my allowance I went down to the hobby shop and bought Nell a plastic model of a Cessna 340.

"This is a good way to learn about airplanes," I said. "If you still want to, I mean."

Nell was standing at the kitchen sink washing some of the breakfast dishes. She wiped her hands on a dish towel and took the model from me and and looked at it. "I still want to," she said. "Will you help me?"

"Sure," I said. "It's easy. You'll see. All it takes is a little patience."

———

We spread newspapers on the picnic table. I opened the box and dumped all the pieces out. Nell sat next to me and we started breaking all the airplane parts off the plastic spine.

"Last summer I put a model plane together out here," I said. "And Junior Hollinger sat right where you are and gave me all this advice I didn't even want."

"Gib says you and Junior aren't speaking to each other anymore."

"I swear, everyone in this neighborhood thinks Junior and I are married or something! You just have to know Junior to understand how easy it is to get sick of him."

"Does he hang around you a lot?"

"All the time. Especially when I don't want him to."

"Sounds like he has a crush on you."

"A crush!" I started laughing; then the more I thought about it, the less funny it seemed. "Maybe you're right," I said.

When we'd finished the frame of the Cessna, I left Nell alone a few minutes to get us a couple of lemonades. When I got back, I hardly recognized the airplane.

"Lord, you've got the vertical stabilizer glued to the nose!" I said. "You'd crash in a second if you flew in this plane—"

"I just can't figure out these instructions," Nell said. "They might as well be written in Martian."

"I never bother with the instructions—they just mix me up. Here." I yanked the stabilizer off the airplane nose. "You just kind of have to know where things are. I'll explain it to you as we go along."

By the end of the afternoon the plane was finished, and Nell could point out the fuselage, the ailerons, the fuel tanks, and the rudder.

"You did pretty good for a first lesson," I said. "Wait'll Gib sees it."

Nell picked up the airplane and looked at it. "It is pretty, isn't it? Is this the kind of plane you want to fly someday?"

"I want to take lessons in that Piper Cherokee out at Mitchell Field," I said. "But someday I want to fly big jets—like a 747 or something."

"Maybe you'll take me for a ride when you get your pilot's license."

"Well, sure," I said. "I'll fly nice and steady so you won't get airsick."

Nell laughed. She held the Cessna up and the sun glinted on its plastic wings. We stood there together for a minute and admired the work we'd done.

"Not bad," I said. "Not bad at all."

29

The next morning I fixed myself a bowl of Rice Krispies and walked barefoot out onto the porch. My idea was to have a nice peaceful breakfast all by myself. That was my idea, but I was in for a surprise: Kate, my mother, and Nell were on the porch swing, their feet up on the railing, just like the other time.

"Looks like everyone had the same idea *I* did," I said.

"One nice thing about this swing," Nell said. "It's built for four."

So I went over and sat down next to Nell. She had a basket of hair curlers in her lap and was just finishing winding her hair up. Kate and my mother each had a cup of coffee. I hooked my feet over the railing like everyone else and balanced my Rice Krispies on my stomach.

"Your mother was just telling me how she and your dad met at college," Nell said.

"Oh, yeah," I said. "I think I've heard that story a few thousand times."

My mother shook her head. "You've only heard it a few *hundred* times."

"I always think it's interesting how people happen to pair up," Nell said. "Like . . . I wonder if you would have met Pokie and Gib's father if you'd gone to a different college."

"I don't know," my mother said. She took a sip of her coffee. "I guess the romantic part of me likes to think I would have. . . . Who knows? Maybe it was meant to be."

"Oh, I love that!" Nell said. "I *love* the idea that two people are meant for each other and will find each other no matter what."

"Wonder who I'll pair up with," I said. "And where he is now."

"I can tell you that," Kate said. "He lives next door to you and his name's Junior Hollinger."

Everyone burst out laughing, and I choked so hard on my Rice Krispies that Nell had to pat me on the back. "Kate, you cut that out now!"

"Well," I heard Gib say. "Look at all of you!" He came bounding up the steps. "I've got to go get my camera—"

"Gib, you will not!" Nell shrieked. She jumped up and put her hands over her head, and the curlers in her lap went flying. Gib ran into the house. "Gib, I mean it! If you take a picture of me like this I'll never speak to you again!"

Gib appeared in the doorway, camera in hand. I yanked my legs down so Nell could get out.

"Gib," Nell said, "I mean it now—"

"Oh, you mean it, huh?" He aimed the camera. "Smile!"

"No!" She ran down the steps, Gib right after her. "Pokie, don't let him!"

I jumped off the porch swing and ran to Gib. He held the camera up high so I started tickling him.

"Hey, this isn't fair!" he said. "Two against one!" I grabbed the camera and tossed it to Nell. Just as he ran to her she snapped his picture, then he threw his arms around her waist and they collapsed on the lawn in a fit of giggles. I was laughing too.

Gib and Nell started drifting into some semiserious kissing when one of our neighbors walked by with her dog. She stopped and stared at them.

"Afternoon, Mrs. Nelson," my mother said. "Lovely weather we're having, isn't it?"

Mrs. Nelson watched Gib and Nell for a couple of seconds, then she looked up at the sky.

"It's supposed to rain," she said, and went on about her business.

Mrs. Nelson may have been shocked, but I was suddenly picking up on something I just hadn't noticed before. Gib was happy.

Happier than I'd ever seen him in his life.

30

That night Nell and Gib cooked dinner for my parents and Kate and me. Spaghetti. How they managed to burn it was beyond me, but they did, so we had to wait while they cooked up a new batch of it.

"I just don't see how you can burn spaghetti," I said. "Even a two-headed monkey can make spaghetti without burning it."

"Not a two-headed monkey who's in love," my father said.

"I'm going to see if I can hurry them up any," I said. "I'm starved."

I went out to the kitchen. Nell was holding a

spoon out to Gib so he could taste the spaghetti sauce.

"I think it needs something," Gib said.

"It doesn't have to be perfect," I said. "You've got a bunch of hungry people out there, you know—"

Nell laughed and held the spoon out to me. "Here. You decide."

I tasted the sauce. "It's fine. How come you're making such a big production out of a platter of spaghetti?"

As I turned to go, I noticed something in the kitchen garbage can: green curls of china. A piece of fuselage, a chunk of wing. Like it had crashed and broken apart.

I looked at Gib. "The airplane bank I made you! Did you break it? What happened?"

Gib looked at Nell, then at me. "I'm sorry I had to break it, Poke, but I needed the money and I couldn't get it out any other way—"

"Oh . . ." I picked up the fuselage and a piece of wing to see if maybe I could glue them back together. "What'd you need the money for?"

"A down payment on this," Nell said. She held up her hand, and I saw a tiny diamond sparkling on her finger.

Gib put his arm around Nell. "We're getting married, Poke."

I dropped the airplane parts back into the garbage can. "Married! You can't get married! You're only nineteen!"

"We love each other, Pokie," Nell said. "We don't want to wait—"

"You're both crazy! Mom and Dad'll never let you do it!"

"Poke, don't get so upset!" Gib said. "I hope Mom and Dad'll be happy about it, but even if they're not, Nell and I are still going to get married."

"It's not fair!" I said. "You were supposed to use that money for your first flying lesson!"

Nell tried to put her arm around me, but I wouldn't let her. "Pokie, I thought you'd be happy for us—"

"You two only think of yourselves! I think you're both very selfish people!"

I ran out the back door. I didn't have anywhere to run to, but then I remembered Junior's rickety treehouse. I ran to his backyard and climbed up on the platform and started to cry. I didn't care if I fell off and broke my neck. I didn't care about anything. Something had shattered between Gib and me, just like the china airplane.

"Poke?" I heard Gib say softly. "Pokie . . . are you coming down or do I have to come up there?"

"I don't care *what* you do anymore," I said.

He climbed up carefully and sat down next to me. "I've been looking all over for you."

"I came up here because I wanted to be by myself."

"Come on, Poke," he said. "Thought you'd be the one person who'd stick by me. Who'd understand."

"You tell Mom and Dad yet?"

"No, I came looking for you—"

"Seems like you've been drifting farther and farther away from me this summer. It doesn't matter how close I get, you're always just out of reach."

"I'm never out of reach," Gib said. "I'm right here. I always *will* be."

I looked over at him. Even though it was dark, I could see his face, his expression. He was worried. About me, I guess.

"You can't help it, Gib. Things will change. They're already changing. You're different now."

"The important things won't change, Poke."

I wiped my eyes with my hand. "What'll you do about college?"

"We'll get an apartment near the campus. Nell's already got a part-time job, and I'll get one, too. Lots of couples do it."

"Guess you won't be taking that flying lesson now."

"Maybe someday," he said. "But not now."

"Yeah."

"Come on, let's go back. I left Nell alone in the kitchen and everyone'll be wondering what's taking dinner so long—"

"You go ahead. I'll be there in a minute."

"You sure?"

"I'm okay. I'll be there in a minute."

Gib reached over and squeezed my hand. "Be careful getting off this thing, okay?"

"I will," I said. "You go ahead."

There was something I had to do. I eased myself down from the treehouse and cut through Junior's yard. He was out on his tire swing, spinning around to make himself dizzy.

"Aren't you afraid you'll throw up?" I asked.

"Hi," he said. "I done this a million times and I never throw up. You know that." He stopped spinning and jumped off the tire. "I saw you out in the backyard during the cookout. I liked the way your hair was, done up in that fancy braid—"

"Why didn't you come over? Your parents were there . . ."

Junior shrugged. "I thought you were mad at me or something."

I stuck one foot in the tire and grabbed the rope. "I didn't mean those things I said that day—"

He gave me a push so I could start swinging. "Me neither."

"Guess what." I said. "Gib's getting married."

"No kidding. . . . Gib's getting married, huh?"

"He's moving to Missouri."

"Wow . . ."

"He and Nell are going to get an apartment near the university."

"You going to miss him?"

I could feel the warm rush of air against my face as the tire swung back and forth. "Yeah," I said. "Yeah. I'll miss him."

Junior didn't say anything. I wrapped my arms around the rope, and he pushed me for a long time.

"Hey, Junior," I said. "I'll take you up to the high school and show you around if you still want me to—"

"Really? You mean it?"

"Sure, I mean it."

"How come you changed your mind?"

"I just forgot for a while," I said. "I forgot what it feels like to have someone leave you behind."

31

"I don't think you and Nell have thought this out at all," my mother was saying. "You're both only *nineteen*—"

I had just walked in the door. My parents and Kate sat on the couch, and Gib and Nell sat on chairs pulled up in front of them. They looked like people in those movies do who are being interrogated by the police.

"We *have* thought about it, Mom," Gib said. "I love Nell. I want to marry her."

My mother ran her fingers through her hair. "All right, but wait a while. Wait till next year—"

"We don't want to wait. We want to get married soon, so we have time to get settled in Missouri before school starts."

"Gib," my father said. "Being married and trying to work and go to school all at the same time . . . do you have any idea what that involves?"

There was a miserable silence.

Kate looked at my parents. "They *don't* know what's involved," she said. "But you two do, because you did it yourselves."

My mother and father looked at each other. Nell put her head down and smiled a little.

"Gib?" my mother said. "Nell? Be very careful what you do, because someday it may come back to haunt you."

The next day Junior and I were having lunch on our back steps. The door was open, and as we ate we listened to the wedding plans being made.

"We'd like it to be a week from Saturday," Nell said. "Gib talked to the county clerk, and that'll give us enough time to get the license and have our blood tests."

"We can't get much of a wedding together by then," my mother said. "There's so much to do—"

"Gib and I thought we'd just get married at city hall—"

"You can't get married that way. . . . Wouldn't you rather have a small ceremony here? Maybe in the backyard?"

"Oh, that'd be great!"

"I better run downtown and see about ordering

some flowers. Do you want to come?"

"I have to call my parents," Nell said. "They don't know yet."

"Tell them they're welcome to stay here if they want."

"Thanks. You've been wonderful."

When I peeked into the kitchen, my mother was gone and Nell was dialing the phone.

"What's she doing, Pokie?" Junior whispered.

"Calling her parents."

"Hey! That's long distance down there to Missouri!"

"Shh!" I said.

"Mama?" Nell said. "Hi . . . how are you? Well, I know, but . . . Mama, I've got some wonderful news. Gib and I are getting married. . . . *Married*. . . . Well, I mean I love him and we're getting married. A week from Saturday. . . . I *do* know what I'm doing!"

"Your parents'll hit the roof when they get the phone bill," Junior said.

I clamped my hand over Junior's mouth.

"If only you'd come up here and meet Gib's family," Nell said. "They're so nice, all of them. His mother wants you to stay here with them when you come up—"

Junior pulled my hand down. "One time my Aunt Bertie visited us and ran up a hundred-dollar long-distance phone bill. I thought my pop would explode when he found out—"

"Shut up!" I whispered.

"We're *not* dropping out of college," Nell said. "We're going to live off campus and work—"

"My pop wanted to sue Aunt Bertie but my ma talked him out of it," Junior said.

"Well, all right, I guess," Nell said; then we heard the phone being hung up. We also heard what sounded like Nell crying.

"I better go talk to her," I said.

"Want me to come along, too?" Junior asked. "I'm real good at cheering people up."

"No . . . no, this is girl talk. You stay here."

Nell was sitting on the kitchen counter, drying her eyes with the end of the paper towel roll.

"Nell? Hey there, Nell . . . what's wrong?"

"Pokie," she said. "It's my parents. They think I'm too young to get married, and they won't come to the wedding."

"Well, they'll make up with you," I said softly. "Maybe . . . maybe once you're married and down there in Missouri, they'll visit you and see how happy you are."

"I don't know. . . . Mama says . . . she says I'm on my own now."

Nell was getting married and her own parents wouldn't come. I thought about *me*, how empty it would feel if *my* mother and father wouldn't come to something that mattered the world to me, like my first solo flight. They had always stood behind me and always would. I never had to worry about my parents cutting me loose out into the world like Nell's had.

"You've still got us," I said. "We'll look after you."

"Yeah?" Nell said softly. "You really feel that way?"

"Course I do. You're part of *our* family now."

Nell smiled and nodded. I slid up on the counter and sat next to her. I just had the feeling that if I were her, I'd like to have someone sit with me for a while.

Someone who cared.

32

Two of Nell's college girlfriends came up from Missouri to be her bridesmaids. One was tall and one was short, and they were both named Peggy. I had never met two Peggys in a row like that.

My mother and I took Nell and the Peggys to the mall to shop for bridesmaid dresses.

"Did you see that bridal gown in the window?" I asked Nell. "It costs over nine hundred dollars!"

"I couldn't afford anything like that," Nell said. "Your mom's letting me wear the gown she was married in."

Nell looked at a bald mannequin who was wearing a light-yellow bridesmaid dress.

"I wanted you along to try on dresses, too,

Pokie," she said. "Because you're going to be my maid of honor."

"Me!"

"If you want to."

"I'd like to be your maid of honor," I said. "I don't have to memorize anything, do I?"

Nell laughed. "No. Just stand next to me and be my moral support."

"I can do that, I guess."

Nell decided on a lime-sherbet-green bridesmaid dress, a dress covered with one thousand ruffles. While Nell was busy with the Peggys, I took the dress over to my mother and showed it to her.

"Do I *have* to wear this?" I whispered to my mother. "I'd rather wear that blue dress I have in my closet. It doesn't even have one ruffle on it, and it looks much better."

"I think Nell wants her bridesmaids to be dressed alike, don't you?"

"If it were *my* wedding, I'd let everybody wear whatever they felt comfortable in."

"When *you* get married, you can let your bridesmaids wear bathing suits and tennis shoes if you want. But this is Nell's wedding, remember."

"Maybe I'll just mention the blue dress—"

My mother smiled. "Maybe you won't," she said, and I came home with the green dress.

The wedding was two days away when Gib started packing up his room in cardboard boxes. I stood in the doorway and watched him empty his bookcase.

"Hey there," I said. "Need any help?"

"Hi. . . . You can hand me some of my books—"

I handed him a stack of paperbacks. "How come you're doing all this now?"

"Won't have time after the wedding. Nell and I are leaving for Missouri right after the ceremony. We're renting a U-Haul and driving down."

"Oh . . ."

"We've got to get down there as soon as possible and find a place to live before school starts."

"Well, I guess . . . I guess I won't be seeing you again for a long time, then."

Gib looked at me. "I guess not."

I felt my eyes get wet. I turned away from him.

"Poke, don't . . ." He stood behind me and wrapped his arms around my shoulders. "Why don't we spend the afternoon together. Let's do something. Just the two of us."

"Like what?"

"Think you have enough saved up for that introductory flying lesson?"

I turned around and looked at him. "I think I have enough in my coffee-can bank—"

"Well, go get it and I'll drive you out to Mitchell—"

"Now? You mean it?"

207

"Sure. Right now."

I threw my arms around him. "I'll go get my bank."

"Looks like good flying weather," Gib said. He pulled the car inside the airport gate and parked next to the No Trespassing sign. "You nervous?"

"Shoot, what's there to be nervous about?" I opened the car door. "I'll go find Hank Jellies. You stay here. Don't go wandering around like you did that time with Nell."

I found Hank Jellies in the airport office. He was leaning back in his chair, talking on the phone, and eating a triple-decker sandwich. He motioned for me to come in. I looked around the office while he finished his phone call. The Piper Cherokee model I'd made last year stood on his desk, right next to the newspaper clipping of Hank Jellies coming home from World War II.

He hung up the phone and smiled. "Well . . . look who's here."

"I want to know if you can teach a flying lesson this afternoon," I said. "I've got the seventy-five dollars—"

He took a bite of his sandwich, then he had to talk sideways because his mouth was full. "Is it okay with your parents if you spend all that money on a flying lesson?"

"It's not for me. It's for my brother. He's getting married and I want to give him a flying present."

Hank Jellies laughed. "A flying present, huh?"

I took the lid off the coffee-can bank and showed him the money.

"Well, wait a second there," he said. "Tell you what." He stood up and put on his sunglasses. "You keep your money and use it for your own flying lesson. I'll take your brother up for free."

"No," I said. "This is something I want to do on my own."

He nodded. "Know what? You're an independent woman, just like my wife." I counted out the seventy-five dollars, smoothed them, and handed them to him. He put the money in a metal cash box. "All right," he said. "Let's go find your brother."

Gib was sitting on the roof of the car watching the planes land.

"Hey, Gib," I said. "Hank Jellies is going to give you a flying lesson."

Gib smiled. "What?"

"Your sister's just paid for your first flying lesson, young man. How about it?"

"Poke . . . we're here for *your* flying lesson, not mine."

"Please, Gib," I said. "You might not get another chance to be a pilot. Not for a long time, anyway."

Gib cleared his throat. He looked very pleased. "I don't know what to say, Poke. I just don't know what to say."

"You don't have to say anything. Just get going, okay? I'll sit here on the roof of the car and watch you."

Hank Jellies handed Gib a clipboard. "That's your preflight check list," he said. "Let's start with the left wing and work our way around the plane."

I climbed up on the car and sat on the roof. I watched Gib and Hank Jellies walk to the plane and start inspecting it. Gib looked like he was having the time of his life. He was going to be a real pilot, even if it was only for an hour. He checked the fuel tanks, the edges of the wings, the ailerons, the fuselage.

When he and Hank Jellies were finished with the preflight, Gib gave me a wave and they climbed into the Piper Cherokee. They sat there awhile; I guess there were plenty of things to check inside the plane, too. I fingered the little silver airplane dangling from the necklace Gib had given me and waited.

Suddenly the engine started.

The propeller spun.

The plane taxied down the runway going faster and faster and faster and faster, until all of a sudden I noticed it wasn't touching the ground. My heart was pounding hard; I wondered how Gib's was doing. I put my hand against my eyes and watched the little Cherokee take off into the sun.

I watched until the plane got smaller and smaller, until it was just a dot, until it had disappeared. The flying lesson lasted over an hour. I didn't have any trouble figuring out which plane was Gib's when he came back.

He circled the field.

Low.

Twice.

Twice, so I would notice him.

33

Nell picks up the veil. My mother's veil. She fixes the headpiece on her head but gets it all crooked, so I straighten it for her.

"I guess I'm starting to get nervous," she says. "Look . . . my hands are shaking."

"Shoot, Gib's no one to be scared of—you know that."

"I know," she says. "I just hope I don't do anything stupid during the ceremony, like trip or sneeze or something."

"Nothing's going to happen," I say. "I'll be right there beside you. I'll catch you if you fall and hand you a hankie if you sneeze."

Nell laughs. "I think you're going to make a

212

very good sister-in-law."

I suddenly feel shy inside. "I never told you this," I say. "But I think Gib's very lucky you're marrying him."

"Thanks, Pokie." She puts her arms around me and gives me a hug.

There's a timid little knock on the door. "Hey there, Gib's girl?" I hear Junior ask in a confused voice. "I'm looking for Pokie. Her ma said she might be in there—"

Nell looks at me and smiles. "There's no one named Pokie in here," she says. "Only Alwilda."

"Alwilda!" Junior echoes. "Who's that?"

I open the door. "Me," I say. "I'm Alwilda now."

"Wow! You really look pretty!" Junior says. "Hey, Pokie . . . I hate to tell you this, but there are a couple of other girls in the hall who have the same dress on as you—"

"I'm a *bridesmaid*, Junior," I say. "We're supposed to be dressed alike."

"Oh, yeah . . ."

"What'd you come up here for?"

"Gib's downstairs. He says he has to see you before the wedding starts."

I look at Nell. "I'll be back in a minute, okay?"

"You go ahead. I'm fine."

Gib stands in the kitchen, peeking out the window at the wedding guests. Kate and my mother have done a nice job with the backyard. White

213

wooden folding chairs rented at the Party Palace are set up in neat rows. Flowers are arranged by the big maple tree, where Gib and Nell will take their vows.

"Hi," I say. "Junior says you wanted to see me."

Gib turns around. "Well," he says. "Look at you . . ."

"Do I look okay? I've never had a long dress before."

"You look all grown up," Gib says.

"So do you."

Gib laughs. "I'm *supposed* to be grown up. I'm getting married."

"You nervous?"

"I'd be lying if I said no." He looks at me for a second. "I wanted to give you something." He pulls an envelope out of his suit-coat pocket and hands it to me. "Dad helped me out on this. Nell and I want you to come down and visit us after we get settled."

Inside the envelope is an airline ticket to St. Louis, with a connecting flight to Columbia, Missouri.

"It's an open ticket so you can come anytime," Gib says. "You'll be our first guest."

I look at the ticket, then at Gib. "Thanks." There's so much more I want to say, but the words just won't come. I settle for giving him a quick hug.

A whirl of activity in the next few minutes: Gib

214

goes outside and my parents follow. I'm upstairs, shooing Junior out of the way, helping one of the Peggys find her shoes, straightening Nell's train, and getting us all downstairs and lined up in the right order. The guests are all seated; it won't be long now. We're to wait inside, until the flute lady starts playing the Wedding March.

While we wait, pictures of past summers come flooding back to me: Gib, teaching me to ride my two-wheeler, to swim, taking me to the carnival, letting me drive our car, helping me hit a baseball clear over the backyard fence. Now Gib stands by that same fence, waiting for his bride, and I don't think summers will be the same from now on.

Outside, the flute lady starts playing delicate notes. The guests quiet. Nell and the Peggys and I walk slowly outside.

I was worried about Gib before. Before I understood how it was between him and Nell. Now, as the Peggys and I step off to one side, Nell stands next to Gib and he sees only her. Not me, or anyone else. That's the way it is now.

Nell hands her bouquet to me—a beautiful bouquet made up of summer roses from our garden. Gib slips the ring on her finger. This is it! I feel an awful tug inside me, like Gib's being pulled right from our family. Then, just after he says "I do" and right before he kisses the bride, his eye catches mine and he gives me a wink.

I feel a smile coming up right from my toes.

Mom and Dad's son.

Nell's husband.

My brother.

We'll always be brother and sister. Nothing will ever change that. Not ever.

Ah, I think later, as Nell tosses her bouquet and it makes a perfect arc in the summer sun, *what a day for the wedding!*